Belmont STORY REVIEW

EDITORIAL STAFF

EDITOR
Sara Wigal

CO-MANAGING EDITORS
Journey Mathewson
Tricia LaMorte

SUBMISSIONS COORDINATORS
Sunny Urben
Mary Louise Whitfield

COPY EDITORS
Dylan Homan
Anna Louise Janes
Cameron Jones
Isabella Kelley
Kylee Ludwig
Madison Perry
Tia Tkachenko

SOCIAL MEDIA
Director: Vi Hendrix
Abigail Eaton
Hannah Webster
Mary Louise Whitfield

POETRY
Director: A.J. Bowen
Tricia LaMorte
Cayla Rusielewicz
Randi Smith

ART TEAM
Kenya Canady
Mary Ciarrocchi
Shanti Liu
Carley Martin
Julia Niden
Hailey Pankow
Zoe Spangler
Kelsey Watson

FORMER MANAGING EDITOR
Richard Sowienski

Email: belmontstoryreview@gmail.com
© 2024 Copyright Belmont University

[TABLE OF CONTENTS]

FOREWORD	4	
POETRY	6	All This While We Don't Notice by Alyssa Stadtlander
FICTION	8	What We Will Become by Ashley Bao
POETRY	24	Equinox by Nathanael O'Reilly
FICTION	26	HB Pencils and a Staedtler Mars Plastic Eraser by Serena Paver
FICTION	40	Miss Helmet-Head by M.K. Opar
NONFICTION	52	My Family Reunion by Belinda J. Kein
POETRY	56	Museologies by Rebecca Pyle
FICTION	58	Jersey Devil by Kelsey Myers
POETRY	78	Mosaic II by Muiz Ọpẹ́yẹmí Àjàyí
NONFICTION	80	To Cut the Rot from the Fruit by McKenzie Watson-Fore
POETRY	92	Yellow Prayers in the Fall Wind by Eli Coyle
CONTRIBUTORS	94	

[FOREWORD]

Usually when I write the foreword to *Belmont Story Review*, it is sometime in late spring, and we are rushing to complete a volume of this magazine. The students are immensely proud each year, and feel accomplished after sifting through the 1000 or so submissions we get annually (and that is with putting a limit on how many submissions we receive). I must write this foreword quickly, within a week or two, even though I haven't learned of the theme of the magazine until we are done selecting each piece of poetry and prose. At that point, the managing editor and I meet to discuss what we think the theme of the volume should be. Our theme's *emerge*—they are not chosen in advance, and that makes the editorial work somewhat mystical, or more obviously mystical, for this type of work is always an alchemy anyway.

This year, many things have changed. For the first time, our annual volume will come from the efforts of two semesters of work, rather than just the spring semester. We will wrap up volume nine in the fall semester of 2024 (instead of the spring prior), and begin volume 10 earlier than normal, in that same semester. Instead of a rush to the finish, the completion of this magazine felt leisurely by comparison. We selected our works and celebrated, but did not rush into the production process as we had for all volumes previously.

Another change is that I am writing this foreword to you at the end of the summer, long after class is completed. I have not seen my students for months, but I will see many of them in just a few weeks when the new semester commences. I have not seen these poems or stories for months either, but today read them with fresh eyes, like a student I had in a class one time, and then did not see again for several years until one day, they say hello in the halls, and I brighten at their kind greeting, and it takes a beat to remember them. When I do it is by a turn of phrase they used in an assignment, or some sweatshirt they wore frequently that I can picture in my head, or the piercing in their nose that I noted because it is similar to mine. Little familiarities in the seemingly foreign.

In my life I have followed the theme of *passage* which in retrospect seems prophetic. There is always this magic to BSR— the students chose the works which give us the theme, and then I find myself noticing it in my own life. This year has been a passage for my career, for my home life, for everything it seems that I feel about myself— and I find myself here on the precipice of *new* along with my students, holding joy and trepidation equally. The process of moving through, past, or away is something that college students and faculty are surrounded by—each student is on their own journey, and we greet them at what seems the start, but for some may only be the middle of their college career. We faculty say goodbye at what feels like the end, but as I have come to know by staying in touch with alumni, it is only the beginning of a new passage on which they embark.

Each passage we move through in life only dumps us out into the next leg of the journey, and here in this little volume of literature, you may find the story to help you navigate yours.

Happy reading,

Sara Wigal, Editor

[POETRY]

All This While We Don't Notice

By: Alyssa Stadtlander
after Denise Levertov's poem, "Window-Blind"

*Much happens when we're not
there*, she writes, like that tree
that falls in the silent woods,

spreading her seeds that slip
under the soft topsoil, layers
of fallen, dying things returning

to their promised
beginnings, her soul wandering
in through the windows

of the leaves who are trying
to grow well again—and all this
while we don't notice.

After, during long sunsets
and snowfalls, there is the enduring
murmur of the seed breaking

open, no roots yet, like a dream
in which you are nearly
awake, stirring while the wakening

sun trickles in
through half-drawn blinds. See? God is not
in the treetops, but crouched

close by in the dirt.

What We Will Become

Ashley Bao

[FICTION]

Florence arrives on Daniel's doorstep at half past six in the evening, the commuter train from Medford to Lowell having been delayed two hours by a derailed freight car. A scarf wrapped around her face protects her against the cold blasts of winter wind, but nothing can prevent the bitter air from seeping through the fabric of her jeans and wriggling through her skin before settling into her bones.

When Daniel texted her two days ago asking to see her so they could try to make things work, she booked the train tickets instinctually, like an old habit. But they haven't truly spoken in a month, the longest they've ever gone without communication since they met. In the grand scheme of things, four and a half weeks is barely anything, but still, she wonders who lives inside the skinny townhouse in front of her, if it is the same person she has known since college. She knocks on the townhouse door with a partially frozen fist, and it opens.

Warmth spills out and there he is. Daniel, her boyfriend of seven years, stands in his entryway next to an Amazon shoe rack and vintage coat hooks. He wears a Boston University sweatshirt and gray sweatpants, both of which are pilling aggressively in the legs and almost worn out in the waistband. They must be approaching seven years old at this point, a remnant of his collegiate days.

In the time since Florence has last seen him in person, Daniel's hair has grown to untenable lengths, giving him baby bangs in the front and the beginnings of a rat tail in the back. He is wearing his glasses, a rarity since he switched over to contacts after graduation. They frame his eyes like little saucers, the kind that teacups clatter against in antique cupboards. It all makes Florence nostalgic for when they were still in college, and she can't help but smile from ear to ear. She knows she looks silly with her cheeks and ears so red from the cold that they look like unpopped pimples, yet she doesn't mind looking silly to Daniel.

After a moment, Daniel smiles back; the bottoms of his eyes crease warmly while his cheeks flush with what Florence hopes is happiness. He holds out a hand and Florence takes it, stepping into the warmth of the house. As he closes the door, Florence buries her face into his chest, wrapping her arms around his torso. His sweatshirt smells like laundry detergent, the kind Florence has long associated with the feeling of "home."

"I missed you," Florence says, words muddled in the fleece folds of Daniel's sweatshirt.

Daniel wraps his arms around her, kissing the top of her head. "Missed you too."

🍂

Daniel has a buffet of takeout Korean food laid out on his small kitchen table. Tteokbokki and kimchi jjigae are laid out in their aluminum tins, red sauces still gurgling from residual heat. A platter of kimbap sits next to the other dishes, cool and cleanly cut.

Bare white walls surround them, newly painted and never marred. Daniel doesn't cook, so he doesn't spend any more time in the kitchen than he has to, at least that is what he told Florence a few months ago when he bought the place. Florence told Daniel he ought to put some paintings up or at least incorporate some color into his interior design, but he wasn't interested. Once the house was livable, it was finished.

Daniel nearly hits his head on the hanging light as he sits in his chair. The house has always been a little small for him, something Florence warned him about when he bought it six months ago. The ceilings are only ever seven feet at their highest and all of the light fixtures hang down from chains on the ceiling. This colonial townhouse wasn't made for a six foot tall man, even one that likes to slouch most of the time.

Florence likes the hanging lights. In an otherwise barren house, they give the rooms dimension, breathing warmth into every dusty corner. Though incandescent bulbs are terribly energy inefficient, their light flickers like beating butterfly wings. The rhythmic movement is comforting.

Without saying a word to each other, they begin to eat. Florence fumbles with her chopsticks to pick up the slippery rice cake. She's self-conscious that she never learned the proper way to hold chopsticks and makes an effort to correct herself whenever she eats with Daniel, whose technique is impeccable. After a few minutes of only hearing the sound of chewing and slurping, Florence sets down her bowl.

"You know, I read a new book recently," Florence says to break the silence. After a month apart, she is rusty at dinner table banter. She's not sure what will spark Daniel's interest, but literature is a reliable topic. "Sally Le's new poetry collection: *Where Silence Ends*."

Daniel looks up from his bowl in acknowledgement. "Was it any good?"

"Very visceral and prose-like. References Ocean Vuong a lot."

"So do all the other Gen Z Asian American poets."

"Well, I liked it."

"You do like Ocean Vuong."

"Don't be facetious to make a point. You keep his first collection in the drawer of your nightstand."

Daniel smiles, his grin slightly lopsided. Florence knows she is the only person who talks to him about poetry. It makes her feel special, having this little piece of him that is only hers.

When they were in college, a time that felt like a lifetime ago despite it only being five years since graduation, they would sit together and read poetry together in Daniel's dorm room. His roommate was always out partying, so late at night the two of them would share a bottle of the cheapest white wine that Daniel's older brother could buy and read. Daniel was more into nineteenth-century white men that Florence would've predicted. He had most Walt Whitman poems half-memorized and copied a stanza of a different John Keats love poem in every birthday card he ever gave Florence.

He wrote poems too, but those were kept secret. Only Florence had ever read them despite her insistence that he submit them to magazines to publish. Florence liked to write too, so she could recognize superior talent when faced with it. If she could manage to eke out a side gig as a mediocre artist at best, Daniel could become great. But he decided to become a chemical engineer for the job security.

Once Daniel finishes his food, he stands up, and Florence thinks he is going to come over and wrap his arms around her shoulders. She thinks he is going to kiss the top of her head and suggest they head to his bedroom with adoration in his eyes. She thinks that things are back to normal since the last time she visited. Instead, Daniel goes to sit on the plain white mid-century modern couch Florence suggested he buy and starts to read a book on ornithology, the spine of the tome as thick as a fist.

But Daniel isn't a conversational person anyways. Florence knows that about him and part of loving him is accepting his personality. So she ignores the mild stab of indifference and finishes her meal. The kimchi is too aged for her taste. It's so plump with brine that all she tastes is the sour ferment.

☙

For their fifth anniversary, Daniel had surprised Florence with a trip to Acadia National Park. They went in summer, when the cliffs were teeming with mosquitoes and tourists. Florence had expected Daniel was going to propose. They were twenty-six which was a perfectly reasonable time for marriage. They'd already started receiving wedding invites from their college friends.

So when Daniel took her on a secluded, relatively unpopular hike in the park, Florence thought that was it. While she was panting, telling him to slow down so she could keep up with him, she thought that the seven-mile uphill battle to get up this stupid mountain would be worth it. The view would be beautiful and the ring would be too.

Eventually, they made it to a clearing. They were surrounded by spruce trees filled with light green summer needles, and Florence felt like a child as she plucked a handful off the branches and threw them into the air like confetti. Daniel laughed as Florence threw some onto his head, and the sound exhaled into the empty forest, rippling through the tree canopy. Then, they kept hiking, took a selfie at the peak, and hiked down.

Looking back, Florence knows that it was silly to think he was going to propose. Not with her having ruined the first night of their trip by sobbing in the cabin bedroom's scratchy comforter after having received another rejection, this one from an agent who had told her before, at a coffee chat, that her first chapter was good. Against all rationale, she had pinned unreasonable hopes on this one man who now became one more person to tell her she wasn't good enough. She knew she was being ridiculous, that she could still submit, that she could still keep writing. But it didn't stop her from breaking down and crying for hours into a scratchy pillowcase. Daniel had wrapped her in his arms like he always did during her outbursts, whispering "I love you's" into Florence's oily, unwashed hair while she blubbered apologies for her emotional volatility. Daniel listened silently. He was so stolid, always holding her when she couldn't hold herself.

Florence was working on herself. She had a therapist; she had tried a dozen medications. But it wasn't working the way she wanted it to. Daniel understood, of course. He always told her he wasn't asking her to change, that he loved her the way she was.

Florence has been trying to convince herself of that fact for the entirety of their relationship to little success. Her therapist says it's because she has low self-esteem and that her defense mechanism is to believe the worst in other people. But Daniel's not going to be able to deal with her much longer, and when he leaves for good, Florence is going to have to deal with herself by herself, a proposition that scares her so much she begins to physically tremble. When she is alone, what will she become?

❧

When Daniel heads to bed, Florence follows. Even after six months of living here, his bedroom is still sparsely furnished, all the furniture bought from IKEA and haphazardly assembled just enough that nothing was in danger of breaking. The bed sheets are tucked under the mattress, the comforter a perfect square quilt on top of the frame. The only signs of life in the room are the couple dozen pages of a manuscript laid out on his desk.

It's the book Daniel had been working on since college, *The Tiger*. Based on the parts she read a few years ago, it's part-poetry part-prose and riffs off of Ken Liu's *The Paper Menagerie* to examine the complexities of the

Wasian experience. It was good, but clearly needed some workshopping on a few of the characters, a critique that nearly blew up their relationship right after graduation. Once Daniel started working, Florence assumed that he had stopped writing. But clearly, she was wrong.

"You're working on *The Tiger*?" Florence asks, picking up a page.

"No, it's just a work thing. Some patent paperwork," Daniel replies as he takes the paper out of her hand. Deftly, he shuffles it back into the pile of pages and tucks them into a drawer. He smiles at her without his eyes. "So, how's your writing going?"

He's retreating from the question again, Florence thinks. Daniel has a tendency to avoid answering questions that he thinks Florence won't like the answer to. So he switches the topic to something safe. He does this because he loves her, so he's told Florence a thousand times before. He doesn't want to upset her because seeing her upset upsets him. But Florence knows when Daniel is hiding things, and she knows how to pry them out.

Florence wraps her arms around Daniel and together they tumble onto the bed. She finds herself a home in the nook of his elbow, intertwining their legs together. His heartbeat pulses against her wrist as she lazily wraps her arms around his neck. He reciprocates, deeply breathing in the scent of her hair. Florence closes her eyes, soaking in the warmth of his body. She traces his jawline with the tips of her fingers.

"Are you working on the book?" Florence asks again as she tilts her head up and forces Daniel to look at her straight in the eye.

Daniel nods, his expression carefully neutral. Florence wonders what he is thinking about when he looks at her.

"Daniel, are you working on the book?" Florence asks for the third time.

"Yes," he says.

A beat.

"I've been editing it for the past month or so. I found an agent." The words come out with extreme reticence, like Florence has placed a gun to his head. "We just got a deal with Penguin Random House. It's going to get published. I'm very happy."

He makes this revelation with no hint of happiness in his voice. His face is still as a statue.

Florence takes a deep breath. Her shoulders begin to tremble.

Florence is a copywriter by day, short story writer by night. She slaves over her work with the kind of perfectionism only going to a school with

English professors who sniffed out flaws like bloodhounds could develop. Her parents are disappointed, she knows. She barely makes enough money to live in a Boston suburb with a roommate. There isn't really a clear upward trajectory for her job, and through the years of failure, she has been made well aware that she is not the kind of writer who has the work ethic and/or talent to break into the publishing world. But she continues; she's been writing a novel for the past three years. Every day, she sits down to edit it, to send it out to agents, to beg her colleagues to nepotism her out of the slush pile. Has she gotten anywhere? No.

Tears leak from her eyes and every breath just gets shakier and shakier. She pushes her head into the pillow to muffle her cries. She wants to turn into Daniel's chest, cry into his shirt like she always does. She wants to roll out of his embrace and never touch him again.

"Why do you always get what you want? It's not fair," she wails. She sounds like a child.

"Do you want me to leave?" Daniel asks, his voice soft and gentle and stoic like it always is when he has to comfort her.

Florence shakes her head, trying to take deep breaths to calm herself. But she hiccups and the spasm in her chest starts another round of tears. Everything hurts, so she hits her legs, punching them so that the little jab of pain can take her mind off of the fact that her life is falling apart. Before she can hit them again, Daniel grabs her hands and holds them still.

"Please don't hurt yourself," he says, his voice straining. Then, he wraps her in his arms and lets her cry it out.

"I'm so sorry," Florence whimpers, guilt and shame squeezing sobs out of her chest. "It's just that I work so hard, but you get everything so easily. Or at least that's how it feels. I know you work hard too."

Daniel stays silent and just holds her tighter. He softly sings some song Florence doesn't recognize even though she thought she knew all of his favorite songs. Still, his voice hasn't changed, so Florence settles in between his gravelly syllables and closes her eyes until the hurt ebbs and sleep lends a veil over her buzzing body.

⁂

The last time Florence visited Daniel, he told her that they should take a break.

They had been washing the dishes, cleaning up after dinner, when Daniel casually said he had something important to tell Florence.

"What is it?" Florence asked, rinsing the leftover starch from the rice cooker.

"I've been thinking that maybe the relationship right now isn't what I want." He dries a fork with a kitchen towel Florence had bought him as a housewarming gift.

Florence blinked.

Daniel explained that he had done a lot of reflection lately and thought that he needed to be by himself for a little bit to better understand his needs and desires outside of the relationship. After all, they had been dating since college. They had been each other's first and only long-term romantic relationship. And isn't that a problem now that they're in their twenties? Maybe they should take a break for a month and then reassess.

Florence blinked again. There was something he wasn't telling her, something he knew would upset her more than being told they should take a break from each other. And because Florence was a masochist, she pried.

"Why?"

And then out came the truth. He had lately felt like she had been too needy. Their nightly phone calls were becoming more of an obligation than something he looked forward to. And he felt emotionally exhausted. When Florence had bad days at work, she would call Daniel, have her emotional breakdowns on the phone and, ultimately, having to listen to her was draining.

Since they started dating seven years ago, Florence had always had the niggling feeling that if they broke up, Daniel would be the one to do it. Even in college, it had always been Florence who stayed over in Daniel's dorm room; it had always been Florence who asked if she could sleepover on late weekend nights; it had always been Florence who felt ignored or rejected if they didn't see or talk to each other one day. Florence cried over their relationship; Daniel watched her cry.

Once they graduated, Florence moved to a city without any of her college friends, and she hadn't managed to find anyone to be more than acquaintances with. She didn't like talking to her parents, so the only guaranteed non-work related social interaction she had in a day was with Daniel. So of course she was going to talk about her emotions to him.

When their relationship went through a rocky patch in their senior year of college—when Daniel had told Florence she was being too clingy—Florence's friends at the time had told her that she was so much hotter and ten times cooler than her boyfriend to try to console her, but Florence had never truly believed them. If that were the case, then why did it feel like she couldn't live without him, but he could get along just fine without her?

But that day, while she washed the dishes, she was determined to act like none of it was affecting her. She shrugged and tacitly agreed.

After they finished cleaning up, they went to Daniel's friend's contemporary dance concert. They sat in adjacent seats. Florence leaned her head against the armrest furthest away from Daniel as she leafed through the program, hoping to understand at least some of the piece. The choreographer wrote that the performance was about communal loneliness.

As the lights dimmed, lithe women in earth-tone chiffon dresses capered about the stage, their bare feet and breaths the only sound that echoed through the theater. At the sound of recorded wind chimes, they began to move, dancing amongst each other but rarely with each other. Despite Florence's reservations, she began to inch closer to the edge of her seat, her eyes fixated on the way the dancers moved like fairies in the floodlights. One by one, across the stage, they flung their bodies backward step by step, always slightly out of time with each other. Florence felt a pit rise in her stomach as she realized that despite sitting next to Daniel, she felt utterly alone in her life.

When Florence told her therapist that she and Daniel were taking a break, her therapist congratulated her. Florence then promptly broke into tears which she assumed would dampen the celebratory mood. But her therapist was unfazed.

"Why is this a good thing?" Florence asked, sniffling. "I thought I was going to marry him."

"Every time you come to a session, you tell me about how something Daniel said or did made you break down."

"It's from work stress and other factors too. It just tends to bubble up when he says something a little off," Florence protested.

"Florence, as your therapist, I think you should be happy in your romantic relationship. And I don't know if you are. So how do you feel about it?"

Florence blew her nose into the scented tissue her therapist always kept on hand. She was upset about the break, obviously. All she wanted to do was curl up in a ball on her couch and cry, which she did until her roommate asked her to please at least cry in her bedroom because she was hosting friends over. She was living in a haze of sadness, the kind that led to her almost crying at Starbucks the day before because the barista misspelled her name.

The saddest part, though, was that she didn't feel any more alone than when she and Daniel were doing great. The grief over the relationship was a familiar taste in her mouth. She had been preparing for it since the first date, since their trip to Acadia, since he shot down her proposal to move in together a few months ago over fear of fostering unhealthy codependency. Her therapist used to assuage her anxieties, tell her that she should do some yoga to feel more present rather than fixating on the future. But Florence had never really listened, so now she is living in a reality she had imagined for seven years. Though they could technically get back together, so really, she was still facing the precipice, staring into the abyss below. It stared back at her.

"I'm terrified," Florence replied, wiping the tears from her eyes. "Really fucking terrified."

In the morning, Florence wakes up before Daniel. For a moment, she looks at his face. He sleeps with his mouth open, jaw unhinged and subject to gravity's pull, drool dribbling down his chin. He shakes his head in his sleep, biting the air occasionally. She wonders what he dreams about; he has never told her what he sees when he closes his eyes.

Then, she slips out of bed as silently as she can. Daniel is a light sleeper, but years together have taught her how to lift the comforter just enough so as not to disturb his temperature-sensitive skin, how to set her bare feet on the floor just gentle enough so as to not creak the wooden boards. She opens the desk drawer, careful not to shake the hinges. She takes the manuscript in both of her hands. Then, cracking open the door just enough to slip through, she walks downstairs to the kitchen. Underneath the watchful white walls, she begins to read.

In college, when Daniel had first started writing this book, Florence remembers the plot being about a half-Korean college student trying to figure out what being an artist really meant. There was a second-generation Korean-American boyfriend who was supporting him, but he was a background character. Mostly, the book was about the narrator's struggle with identity and search for family as he navigated university.

But as Florence skims the book now, she notices how the boyfriend suddenly has a much more prominent role. He is a painter with a lot of talent but a lot less penchant for marketing. He can't make a living from his art, a fact that is slowly destroying him and the relationship. Florence stops on one scene in particular where after a particularly bad art show, Jiwoo, the boyfriend, is upset.

As David held Jiwoo, stroking the other's hair, he said, "It's really hard for me to see you like this. If I'm being honest, that's why I haven't been spending as much time with you anymore. I never know if you're going to start crying out of nowhere.

"I'm not asking you to change, of course. It's just for my own mental health's sake, it's really hard for me."

His face was impassive as he said the words, but Jiwoo heard the quiver in his voice, the small tightening of his fingers as he ran them across his scalp.

In the margins, the agent complimented this section. *Very authentic emotions!* they had written.

Florence doesn't know whether to be flattered or offended that her role in Daniel's life has been mapped onto a gay Korean-American man. Mostly, she is struck by how honest David is, how he says the things he feels towards Jiwoo in the moment he feels them. Florence can't bring herself to keep reading. It feels invasive in a way it never felt when she read the whole thing seven years ago.

So she imagines that the ending has stayed the same. In the original draft, David goes to Korea without Jiwoo in order to find his long-lost grandmother. As a parting good luck gift, Jiwoo gives David a paper tiger folded from a handwritten letter. On the plane to Korea, David unfolds the tiger and reads about Jiwoo's cancer diagnosis and inevitable death. Florence thought the ending lacked the emotional resonance Daniel was going for and told him as much. After all, for the entire story, Jiwoo barely appeared except to comfort David whenever he was sad. He had no character beyond "supportive," and the story spent more time exploring David's friendship with his art professor than his relationship with Jiwoo. So when he died at the end, Florence felt confused as to why she was supposed to care about Jiwoo; the story didn't seem to.

Her suggestion at the time was to expand Jiwoo's character and give him more time in the story at the expense of the chapters of David's internal monologues. That sparked a week-long argument between them. Daniel was quiet except when it came to his writing; they were both defensive about their art. But after so many years, Daniel has taken her advice. Florence thinks the original ending works with this version of the novel: David and Jiwoo are both so self-obsessed that their relationship has deteriorated to the point where they can't even talk about a terminal cancer diagnosis in-person. When David unfolds the paper tiger as he leaves America, he is confronted with the fact that what they had wasn't a relationship; it was convenience.

🐯

Florence first met Daniel in sophomore year of college at an Asian frat party, a place famous for christening true love. Florence had sworn off parties after going a little too hard freshman year, but it was Halloween and her friends insisted. This one would be different, they claimed.

Daniel was a gangly, average height-to-tall Wasian with recently permed hair and gold-rimmed glasses. He looked mildly queer in the dim party light, but was clearly straight upon closer inspection. He held his red solo cup of beer like it was an obligation as he leaned against a wall scrolling on his phone. Just Florence's type. A mutual friend introduced them, and they took a shot of vodka of questionable quality together as a conversation starter.

Chemical engineering major, Los Angeles native, his parents were professors at UCLA, he wanted to be a writer but was now on track to actually make money as long as he could pass organic chemistry. This piqued Florence's curiosity.

"I write too," she said, sipping her third seltzer of the night. Her face had flushed two drinks ago, but she didn't feel drunk yet. "I'm an English major."

"I still write when I can," Daniel responded. His fingers tapped on the rim of his cup. "Do you want to read some of it?"

They exchanged numbers, and he sent the pieces over. It turned out he was a poet. He wrote aggressive poems, the kind that attack the reader with a spear and twist the point into their chest. He asked a lot of questions about race and masculinity, especially regarding his parents. He had one poem where he wrote a letter to his emotionally-absent white father, asking him what kind of son he expected to have. Right to the point, the piece was titled: *Korean or American?* Florence loved most this one line:

appa, i am a reminder of all that you—somewhere under your leaded tongue—know is true but have not yet spoken

When Florence read his works, it was like reading him. She understood that he wished his father had been home more during his childhood, that he wished he spoke Korean well enough to speak to his grandparents, that he was scared of the uncertainty beyond college. The future was calling and he wasn't sure how to answer. His only prose work was this work-in-progress novel that he claimed was no good but Florence could see the pride behind his eyes. Florence devoured his works and asked for more and more. Even then, she supposed she was asking Daniel for more than he thought he needed to give.

He gives lots of things to her now: birthday presents, summer vacations, physical comfort. He's patient with her. He loves her. He really tries to understand her and help her through her emotional outbursts.

Florence explained all of this to her therapist once, and her therapist replied, "What if you need more than just 'trying?'"

Daniel doesn't wake up until Florence has already cooked eggs and toast for breakfast. She is plating the food when he groggily lumbers into the kitchen. The light streaming through the kitchen window catches him at all the right angles, and Florence is compelled to look at him. Spotting her, he flashes a sleepy grin before settling down at the dining table. This is the normal routine of theirs when Florence comes over: she cooks and he does the dishes.

Once the plates are on the table, the two of them sit across from each other. Daniel places a hand on the table, palm facing the ceiling. Blinking in his contacts, he looks at Florence. He wears a polo shirt, the collar unevenly popped around his neck. His hair is gelled back a bit too severely. He looks like a little kid play-acting at adulthood. Florence is under no delusion that she looks any differently with her t-shirt and fluffy pajama pants.

"I love you," Daniel says quietly. It is so sincere.

Florence puts her palm in his, intertwining their fingers together. In Daniel's soft eyes and sharp nose, behind his plump cheeks and thin lips, Florence sees the boy who would invite her to his dorm room on Saturday nights so they could read poetry together. Underneath fairy lights strung up above his lofted twin XL bed, they would get a little too close to each other and pretend that every brush of their hands was an accident. Daniel would read Florence's short stories and tell her he loved her characters, how her dialogue sang off the page, how he was sure she was going to publish and become a successful author. Her heart aches.

"I think we should break up," Florence says.

Daniel curls his fingers on top of Florence's. He opens his mouth for a moment before closing it. He contemplates for another moment before he speaks, successfully this time, "Okay."

Then, for the first time in the seven years they have been together, he starts to cry. At first, Florence only knows he is crying by the shine in his eyes, but then all at once, tears fall onto the kitchen table. His shoulders tremble and his lips contort. Every hiccup wracks his body as he weeps. Snot pools around his nostrils, and he takes his hand from Florence to wipe it with his shirt sleeve. He's an ugly crier.

Florence stands up and walks over to Daniel's side of the table. She wraps her arms around his neck, buries her face in his hair, and holds his sadness in her open palms for the first and last time.

[POETRY]

Equinox

By: Nathanael O'Reilly

When you sit by the fireplace alone
reading Yeats, stare into the black night,
remember the summer evening when you
placed your right hand on my forearm outside the cinema, removed your mask,
declared your love, kissed me in the shadows.
Parked taxi-drivers watched like sentinels
as we caressed, kissed in orange lamplight.
Parakeets tucked heads under their wings,
settled down for the night in the cool air.
A brushtail possum scampered over a fence,
up a tree trunk to the shelter of leaves.
A rummaging in a bin, perhaps a rat,
disturbed our carefully cultivated poise.
We held each other beneath southern stars,
embraced the autumnal equinox.
I remember your sharp white teeth,
distant heels ticking across pavements,
trying to slow down, savour every last
second of our spontaneous self-indulgence.
We did not foresee our undoing
years later in a disintegrating foreign city.

We had no idea how we would feel
in the future, didn't think about the hour
of passion as existing beyond the now.
As you sit by the fire in your snug house
stare into the black night outside and wonder
if my arms are lovelier than aloneness.

Note: This poem is a terminal utilizing the end-words from
Denise O'Hagan's "A World in Waiting."

HB Pencils and a Staedtler Mars Plastic Eraser

Serena Paver

[FICTION]

Summer in London slicks the backs of my knees and pastes my t-shirt onto my spine. The days spread out, slow and ticklish; an ant crawling over exposed skin, the rustle of leaves, the insistent movement of long summer grass, murmuring with gentle new life. A month ago, I visited Richmond Park and walked through its growing mass. Upon returning home, I discovered my sneakers were caked with flaky grass-seed tops. They filled my socks with fluff and found their way between the cracks of my floorboards. Now, a month later, the grass hums and clicks. It ebbs with unseen stories, animation unable to retain its former secrecy. It lulls me into heavy-lidded somnolence. As I listen, something inside my chest clicks and whirs along with the grass, the passing bicycles. A machine winding up before it springs.

This morning, I am on the brink of things. I am waiting for you. It has been five years since I saw you last; your damp, bouncing top-knot disappearing around the sterile white boarding gate of Cape Town International Airport. A pair of exposed, vulnerable shoulders and mop of half-heartedly tamed curls. It is fitting that we should meet here, on this day, when the London weather has surprised us all by peaking at thirty-one degrees Celsius. Any whisper of cloudy moisture has been erased from the sky. The heat unspools like youthful indolence. Like heady days spent lazing on worn out beach towels spread out on your browning lawn, your head resting on my lap, your nose in a book.

When I think of those days now, my mouth tingles with the acridity of unfulfilled passion. It had seemed promised that, if we waited long enough, the world would simply be served to us, twin spirits dying to attend at the altars of Bacchus and Venus. Aged sixteen, we were selfish and irresistible in our pursuit of frivolity, indulgence, pleasure, and love. I used to coil your hair around my fingers and pretend it meant something, the fact that your tight curls were the exact circumference of my ring-finger. That summer of 2011 seemed as tightly coiled, waiting patiently to spring back against anything that stood in its way. Our girlhood itself was a covenant. It was all soft skin and softer thighs. Pencil drawings at the ends of intricately folded letters (school-mandated stationery lists request each student to come stocked with at least four HB pencils), giggles, back tickles, the brushing of hair and comparing of skin tones, my translucent inner wrist against your honeyed mahogany thigh.

Sometimes, I think, I am still on the edge of my girlhood. And I wonder how long this will be allowed for. At what age will it become repulsive for me to giggle like a schoolgirl entering her first love affair? I have never had a *love* affair at all. Maybe that's why I still find a girlhood giggle trapped inside me, coiled tightly at the base of my stomach like a butterfly's tongue. Waiting, as ever. Waiting to be released from the flesh aging around it. It has been 10 years since that summer, but I cannot escape that unfulfilled yearning for an unnameable entity to tear into my soul and fill me with something magnificent; equally as unnameable, but pulsing with life and purpose.

At sixteen, we were not yet suffering with it. We luxuriated in our awkwardness, thinking it a phase. I softly ran my index finger over your upturned palm and made up stories about the lines there, inventing, each time, a more gruesome death lurking in your future. You dissolved into fits of laughter, but your hand closed tightly around mine, and your nails dug into my skin. We talked about boys; practiced kissing on mirrors, and the backs of our own hands, and, one evening, after finishing a bottle of stolen cooking sherry, on each other. Your mouth tasted sharp and acidic. Sometimes, when I wake up, I still have its ghostly aftertaste sitting at the back of my tongue. I loved you then. I felt I knew all the hollow parts of your body. And as we tiptoed along the slippery jetty separating the space allocated to being children from the space allocated to being adults (and I wondered which of us might slip off first), I knew the exact amount of effort it would take for me to shove your beloved/hollow body into unrecognizable womanhood. When you did disappear, you did it gracefully but all at once, without warning executing an Olympic-level dive: somersault, pike, tuck, release.

I felt left behind by you. Often watching from the side lines (pressing down on my well-sharpened pencil until it tore through the paper underneath, lead snapping at the root) as you sampled everything life offered you. Everything other than me. In defiance of you, I decided to leave first. I moved to a town ten hours away, only to study the same degree as you. If this hurt you, you did not let it show. You happily accepted my exits and re-arrivals over university vacations as intervals in your exploration of everything else. I bitterly watched each of your triumphs and heartbreaks, half wanting you to fail and give you a reason to return to your dependence on me.

When I was at school, 832 kilometers away, I lost myself as much as I could. I tried to drown you in two-for-one thirteen-rand double whiskeys and the unremarkable chatter of boys trying to become men. When their hands reached my inner thigh, or the small of my back, I did not try to stop them. But each time the nail of my left thumb would dig circles into any flesh available and leave angry red imprints: half-moons, sleepy eyelids, your coiled hair.

It was easy to get caught up in the agendas of these boy-men. Being boy-men, they never questioned whether their desires would be met. They grew up being satiated and it did not occur to them that any other way of being existed. My own desires (thick, unclear, ebbing, much like the insistent murmur of the Richmond grass I now find myself damp and sitting in) were undefined and could not stand up by themselves. It was easier, always, to go with the assurance of others. I found myself disappearing into people's hands as they brushed past me, sticking to everything, or allowing everything to stick to me, until I, an undefinable sticky mess, eventually had no outline at all, no thick black borders, only insides. Swirling gray pencil lines scribbled, then lackadaisically erased by a white Staedtler eraser.

I used to let the boy-men kiss me. Pull me to them and tangle their fingers in my hair. I used to be hungry for it. Push them against walls, biting and scratching them, opening my mouth wide to swallow them entirely. Their tongues tasted of garlic and ash from cheap cigarettes. And when they slept in my bed their sweat smelt like old meat. We never had sex. No bodily fluids were spilled. But I would wash my sheets immediately after they left, desperate to remove the smell of day-old salami that lingered after their final kiss goodbye. Some would message me after, curious (tempted, challenged by my rejection of their attempts to enter me) enough to believe they were in love with me. Others were happy to never speak to me again, begrudgingly acknowledging me with half nods as I passed them on campus, or in one of the six drinking establishments our small university town offered.

After we finished our matching degrees (our pieces of official paper sporting the same words with different emblems), we celebrated by climbing a mountain and getting drunk at the top. My back ached from lugging up three bottles of cheap, too-sweet sparkling wine and I lost one of the corks in the bushes with an overzealous pop, but I was satisfied. We shared each bottle, sip for sip, drinking in some of each other each time we pressed our lips to the thick rim of the heavy green bottles. Emotion bubbled up inside me and a long-forgotten desire to pull you close began to sting my fingertips. Your head heavy with fake champagne, you fell into me, resting your curls at the nape of my neck.

"I'm moving to London," you told me then. "My family is going and I'm going with. It'll be fun, I guess. A new adventure."

Ice veins. Terror. Something like sparkling wine bubbled the wrong way up my throat and I could not tell if it was vomit or tears. I swallowed it with upturned lips.

"What would you even do there?" I asked.

"Oh, anything. It's London, right? What wouldn't I do?"

We stumbled down the mountain after midnight. The evening summer air cooled my alcohol-flushed cheeks. I lost my balance once and grazed my knee, but you vomited twice, curling your body over into a rounded question mark. So I think I won.

After you left, life became less circular. Straight lines and directness were my concerted focus. I discovered how easy it was to have sex, and could never quite understand why I waited so long to have it. People would ask me about it, eyebrows raised: *twenty-one is quite late, isn't it?* You had sex for the first time when you were sixteen on a Tuesday night with your neighbor's boyfriend. You told me about it the next day as we lined up for the mid-week assembly, proudly poking your tongue out and telling me you didn't bleed. I remember smiling and driving my hands into the faded blue of my threadbare school blazer's pockets, rolling a rescued cut-in-half eraser between my thumb and forefinger. I didn't bleed either, when five years later, I finally just let it happen to me, conducted by my thirty-five-year-old married boss behind the bar we both tended. I imagined myself in love with him, so taken up was I by his adoration of me. An energy which turned out to be disillusionment in the woman he had married seven years prior, who, after having two children and one miscarriage, was fifteen kilos heavier, liked wearing her hair in low, no-nonsense ponytails and no longer performed fellatio. In contrast, I went down on him often and spontaneously, regularly bringing him to climax in less than a minute. Afterwards he would look me in the eye, lightly stroking my face.

"Your skin is so smooth," he would say, trailing his right index finger along the lines yet to form around my mouth. The year he got married was the year I first met you. It was our first year in high school.

I enjoyed sex and decided to have it regularly. First with him, on every vaguely sticky surface our workplace offered us, and then with others, who moved in and out of my life in intervals of varying lengths. Nothing more than shadows, vessels that allowed me to continue my love affair with passion itself. An unrequited love affair.

You and I kept in contact over the years, sometimes talking a lot at once and other times letting months pass without so much as saying hello. Once or twice you called me in the early hours of the morning, unexpected and sobbing, and I talked you through another break up. I imagined your body, still circular, curled like a question mark once more on the floor of your bathroom, your face streaked with makeup, your hair an unruly halo. But our calls became less frequent when you met Tom, a chance encounter as you were exiting Covent Garden station. *He had an aura about him*, you told me on a video call later, something alluring that you couldn't quite put your finger on: *I was feeling some type of way.* He was unshakably British, with tousled brown hair and charmingly cute front teeth, which crossed slightly. He was a meat and two veg, football on Sundays, PG tips, what-you-see-is-what-you-get kind of man. He had moved to London from Newcastle two years prior and worked for a private security company. When you were with him you felt like a woman. Like a complete and well-rounded thing. He made you feel like a step in a set of stairs, part of a routine, warmly included in a life story that had been constructed decades before either of you had been born. More than included — necessary. Needed. Essential. It was a new feeling and it confused you at first. You couldn't work out why you suddenly felt so attached to this man, who was ostensibly unremarkable. *You know, he fucks me right*, you texted me once, *How can I not keep going back for that?*

When he asked you to marry him it did not surprise you. His school friends, by this time, had almost all moved in with their partners, were picking names for their second child, were already celebrating leather, fruit, wood anniversaries. By this time, you understood your presence in his life as a single stair, a small but indispensable part of a greater whole. A structure that was practical, everyday and something that helped elevate him. It seemed right. A worthwhile existence.

Originally, I was invited to your wedding. A countryside affair in the (northern hemisphere) spring of 2020. It was to be a practice run of my own planned eventual move to England. Due to unforeseen but significant worldwide circumstances, your wedding was first postponed, then downsized into a rushed city hall affair in the late summer of the same year. Being a married woman came with its own spirals, and in the year that followed, despite my move to a flat a mere hour away from your Greenwich home, you spun separating circles around a life that I suddenly had no window into. You did not reach out to me after my move. The silence between us was loud enough to muffle even London's barrage of endless noise.

The circumstances were such that I felt anger was unwarranted, but I was resentful regardless. It was a year of disappointment and withdrawal. It felt nobody was safe from becoming drawn into unshakeable domestic isolation. Mine, shattered by a mid-pandemic immigration, was split evenly with strangers from the internet, who shared my west London flat. Yours ended as it began, in the house of your husband, a face-bricked two-up two-down number with a square of grass out back. Autumn turned to winter, to spring, to summer and after one year of married life you woke at two a.m. from a dream about mermaids and texted me immediately.

hey, you said (no punctuation). *i just dreamt about a mermaid whose hair was all the currents in the entire ocean and it kept pulling her head back and she couldnt breathe so she cut it off and then all the fish died*, you said (no punctuation). *sorry... i think i should have messaged you sooner*, you said (an ellipsis). *are you okay*

    I could have messaged you sooner as well. After moving to London, each of my mornings started the same way. I would wake from a nightmare at around 5:30 a.m., watch YouTube for two hours, have Oaties for breakfast, go on a long walk in Richmond Park and start work online at 10. During each of these tasks, though not during my work hours, I would consider sending you a message. I constructed them in my head as I walked from leafless naked tree to leafless naked tree. But I never said anything. I felt too raw from your sudden absence, which somehow seemed new and deliberate, despite us going months without talking before. When I woke at 5:30 a.m. after another nightmare and found your texts waiting, I sat with them for a full day before I responded with (a very well punctuated): *Well, lockdown, you know*. And then after some more thought: *Honestly, I'm better than expected. Are you okay? Wanna hang out?*

    A date was set and, the weather promising, a picnic was planned. A summit on neutral territory. I suddenly felt embarrassed about my cramped and grubby flat, and you did not offer your hospitality at your husband's house. I arrived early, hassled and sweating, and filled with the go-go-go bustle of London. But the sight of the grass moving ever-so-slightly in the breeze first slowed, then stilled me. We had planned to meet at the gate but I felt drawn into the rolling mass, wading through it like shallow water. By the time I sat, sheltered in it, the internal clicking had begun. And here I am again, waiting.

    When you arrive, the first thing I notice is your sun dress. Calf-length and yellow, with a floral pattern, it plays with floating above and below your high-raised grass-wading knees. Your mass of curls surrounds your face, cropped short into a gravity defying circle bob. When you see me you pause, place your hands on your hips.

    "Well, hello gorgeous!" your face spreads wide to expose a smile, an eerie echo of an expression I know well, yet is somehow new and alien now.

    "Let me look at you then!" you say, as I rush to stand and brush myself off.

    Only now do I notice your stomach, a subtle but certain protrusion that does not match the rest of your slender form. I falter, confused. Look at you. Look at it. You notice, place both hands lightly on it and raise your eyebrows at me.

"Yes, it's true, I have picked up a few of them lockdown kilos. Unfortunately for me, it's going to take more than a few visits to the gym to shed them. Gotta wait at least four more months for that."

We embrace. It is too hot and too sticky and simply too awkward, but we don't care. There seems nothing else we can do but pretend nothing has changed at all.

"I guess congratulations are in order!" My cheer is forced, as it often was with your successes. "Let's find somewhere shady to sit, shall we?"

I had brought a bottle of chilled white wine for us to share. Now I find I am the only one drinking it, sipping it slowly but steadily as we catch up. We tell each other the menial things first. How work is going, my new job, your regrettable lockdown puppy, when I am expecting to actually be able to physically enter my office for the first time. This leads naturally into topics that are more emotional. The pandemic, how far we have come, memories (the night we snuck into the school pool, the childhood family holiday you had in Mozambique, the first time I was catcalled at ten years old). As we talk, your hands take turns to rest on your stomach, swapping back and forth, always there but never there at the same time. Each, generously, allowing the other to share its time next to your hidden treasure. You seem to be unaware your hands are doing this, as if they have needs and emotions of their own. It takes an hour and a half for us to circle around to it, the most obvious topic.

"It's going to be a girl, apparently," you say. You look sad when you say it. I can guess why. You haven't yet mentioned your husband by name.

"Have you been thinking about names yet, at all?"

"Not yet. It seems a bit... I mean, *she* seems a bit immaterial right now to be honest. I don't feel a thing when I look at myself naked in the mirror. When people congratulate me, I always wonder what they mean."

"I don't understand." I'm lying on my back now. My head is spinning, enough for me to move in and out of this conversation with distracted heaviness. The leaves on the tree above us rustle, the grass still sings, my lips feel sleepy and resist the motion of my jaw forcing them to make words. The wine bottle, now three quarters empty, lies partially underneath me, the neck sticking into the part where my lower back meets my waist. I can't be bothered to move it.

"I don't know. It just..." you trail off, running your hand over the rough surface of our picnic blanket. "I just feel like I'm stuck in a waiting room."

Waiting. Again. "I didn't think it would be like this."

"What did you think it would be like?"

"I guess, I thought I would feel more impatient or excited. I thought my husband would still look me in the eyes and tell me he loved me, instead always looking down at my stomach. I thought he would still want to have sex."

I roll over onto my side and prop myself up to look at you. "He doesn't? I thought that was his whole thing? I mean, you always spoke about that."

"Yeah, I thought that too."

You don't make eye contact. It was a habit you used to have when you were hiding something you felt guilty about. You were bad at lying then, and you are bad at lying now.

"Tell me my future," you say, abruptly thrusting your left hand out at me. "How am I going to die now?"

I take hold of your hand in mine and press into the flesh of the center of your palm firmly with my thumb. Without looking at the lines that curl and cross there I say, "You'll die aged ninety-nine surrounded by your eleven grandchildren."

You close your hand tightly around my thumb. "Be serious."

"I am!"

"That's not what you used to do. Tell me the truth. How will I die really?"

"You're aware I can't actually read palms, right?"

You pull your hand away. You are still avoiding my gaze.

"I was never sure, to be honest. You were always so good at guessing all of my secrets."

I scoff at that. "That's because we spent everyday together in a tiny town. There wasn't much space to hide."

"London has lots of nooks and crannies."

"Do you make use of them?" I say, boring my eyes into you. You are inscrutable to me now, looking anywhere but my face, your right hand still clutching onto your stomach. I sit up. "Are you trying to hide something?"

You are still and silent, looking out over the seemingly endless park, this impossible green break into the middle of a mass of brown and gray. You are bristling with anxiety of some kind, teetering on the edge of a coin. Heads or tails. Then suddenly you curve forward, pressing your cheek into my lap. In an instant you turn coy, your cheeks flushed. Your face crinkles into an almost giddy smile and I am transported back ten years.

"Oh, I don't know!" you sigh, covering your face. "You're going to think I'm crazy."

I don't say anything. After a while, you look up, rolling onto your back so that you are facing up to me.

"I think I'm in love."

I raise my eyebrows.

"I think I'm in love with a woman."

You are looking up with me with innocence in your eyes. Your feelings transporting you back into a clear-eyed purity. Your eyebrows pucker at me, willing me to understand. I press my finger into the picnic blanket, drawing endless circles which spiral inward, becoming ever more compactly wound. I say nothing.

"She walks her dog along the same route I do. He stole Benji's ball and wouldn't give it back. We got to talking and it just... I don't know how to explain it, something just made sense. I met her a week after I found out about this," you indicate towards your stomach. "Her name is Henri, Henriette. I've never felt like this, I just want to... I don't know, explode or something."

As you tell me about her — *Henriette* — words trip out of your mouth in quick child-like procession, falling over each other, pushing each other forward, pulling the sides of your mouth into an ever-upward growing curve. The edges of your lips are pulled apart from each other, quite unable to help themselves from spreading to show the whites of your teeth, which glisten with saliva. Briefly it crosses my mind that you may still taste the same. All these years later, still sharp and acidic. I wonder if Henriette has tasted you, and if she has, whether or not she likes it.

"I just," you let out a short gasping laugh, "I really fucking like her."

I'm not sure what you want me to say. You look at me as if you want me, in a single sentence, to absolve you of all your guilt and allow you, instead, to just feel joy. I say nothing. Maybe I want you to feel guilty.

"You're disappointed in me," you say. Your eyes are sad. I feel the desperate urge to take an eraser to all the smudges and cross-outs that have marked the last ten years.

I become distracted, considering erasers. Objects, spotless, bought in bulk by middle-school girls, made with the purpose of being dirtied, destroyed, consumed by the task of removing mistakes. As a child, I used to enjoy easing the blue-gray cardboard cover slowly off of my brand-new eraser's body, exposing its unblemished white rubber flesh, and driving my pencil lead deeply into the point at its center. After, I would hurriedly push the cardboard back over the darkened hole there, anxious I had ruined it. When I used the eraser, leaded-hole covered by cardboard, I could not see the damage I had incurred. But I still felt sick sometimes, knowing it was there, unseen, imperfect. I hated that hole, made not with usage but with satisfying spite. Yet, without fail, each new eraser I acquired would receive the same treatment. Now, I look down at my own thighs, untouched by the sun for many months, white and rubbery like the flesh of an unused eraser, and wonder how I might be able to position myself to remove the errors of your life. Am I willing to do that, knowing it means my own, slow whittling away? If I choose to take that role it surely means an unsatisfying end for me. Thinking about it, I cannot remember a time when I finished an eraser completely, rubbed it down to its last crumbs and obliterated it. Erasers get lost, lent out and forgotten. If I try to imbibe your mistakes, perhaps I will simply become an easily-replaceable object. I will not be replaceable to you. I cannot be.

    I lie back down next to you, collapsing myself to fit into your side, pushing my cheek against your shoulder. It will have to suffice as an answer because I have none for you. Together we look up at the stringy white clouds that are beginning to make their triumphant return to the afternoon sky. You lace your hand into mine, future-harboring palms pressed together: your left, my right. I can almost feel the blood pulsing through the tips of your fingers, whirring, ticking, vibrating at the life you see stretched before you. Possibly you simply find yourself in a similar position to me, chasing the unnameable. Your new-found defibrillator — *Henriette* — acting as a promise you will no longer have to wait, another promise, always one more promise, to believe in, to keep the giggles alive, the cheeks flushed, the heart racing, even as it becomes improper to do so. Here we are, two (old enough) women who should have long ago given up on fairy tales, knowing that life is not erasable.

    Perhaps, we feel this way because we were never *allowed* to be children. Because in my living memory I have always been on that jetty-edge, waiting, aware that womanhood was below, wild and seemingly bottomless, just one wrong step away. I would not be allowed a second chance at innocence; no blemishes would be forgiven. At any moment, definitivetely from the age of ten (but, in reality, from a much younger age), my childhood was an expendable thing that just needed to be looked at wrong for it to fall over sideways. Whether it did or did not, in the end, was not the issue, but rather the fact that, from a mournably early age, I was aware of this precarity, and had to take responsibility for ensuring its continued uprightedness. If it did happen to fall (or be pushed over) then that would ultimately have been my fault. I was forced to grow up by the nature of my responsibility to maintain my un-growed-up-ness, and I was not the only one.

    You, too, mourn the unlived innocence that in some way was never offered to you. When your hands wrap softly around the top and bottom of the orb-like protrusion from your middle, they circle it like a crystal ball. Your baby girl's future is written out for her already, her womanhood set in stone by the mere suggestion of her genitalia, which has not yet been fully brought to life. When I see your fingers resting so softly — *so softly* — on your stomach, like the slightest pressure would cause it to deflate, I wonder if maybe the unsatisfied tingling we waded through in our shared youth was not the desire to become, but the desire to *un*become. Not to be an adult at all, but fully a child, safe and carefree. A desire that could never be fulfilled, could only grow more pressing and impossible with each passing day. Our girlhood (ebbing and waiting) coils itself into all sorts of contortions, desperate to be kept alive in bodies that are slowly dying. Making up for the mistakes of the world by the means of its own slow destruction. And we lie side-by-side on our picnic blanket, waiting.

Miss Helmet-Head

M.K. Opar

[FICTION]

Deborah had the courage to cut off her long hair for two reasons: the Miss Teen Bee pageant had come to a close, and her mother was out of town. She had barely crawled out of her evening gown when she had booked the appointment. In the days that followed, she had felt skittish around her mother, almost naughty. But her mother left for Tallahassee oblivious to her schemes, and the day finally came: May 31st, 1969 at 10:00 a.m., the date and time of her emancipation.

"Are you sure?" her hairdresser had said, running her fingers down her strawberry blonde strands. "It's so long."

Deborah had never been surer in her life. She had stuck to her excuse about split ends, *I had to curl it over and over for the pageants. It's so dam-*

aged now, see? Whole inches are fried!

She could have cried tears of joy when the hairdresser chopped it all away. She felt like a snake shedding old skin. This pixie was a symbol of her new birth and courage against her perfect, pageant-obsessed mother. The drive home was even more euphoric; she blasted Nancy Sinatra on the radio, sang along at the top of her lungs, and marveled at her reflection in the rear-view mirror at every stop light. She looked happy. She looked like *herself*. The joy carried her home, but it fled the moment Debby saw her mother's white Ford Galaxie wagon parked in the driveway, two whole days before she was supposed to be back.

Shit.

Every bit of excitement she felt deflated into panic. She was supposed to have more time to build her case, to convince her mother to like the haircut at best and not kill her at worst. What was she *thinking*, doing this without her mother's permission, when her mother wouldn't let her leave the house without checking to see if she had pantyhose on? She was dead. Seventeen years on this earth, and all she had to show for it was a wall of runner-up pageant trophies and two feet of discarded hair. Maybe she could live out of her car. That's what the hippies did, right? Boy, her pastor father and pageant queen mother would sure be proud. *Yes, we spent hundreds on pageant fees and dresses and dance lessons on our daughter, and she is putting it to great use getting high in a field somewhere in Northern California.*

Deborah took a deep breath and looked at herself in the rear-view mirror. Maybe it wasn't as short as she thought. Sure, her mother would notice it, but pixie was too generous of a word to describe it. It's... a very short bob, that's all. It's sassy. It's French, even. It complimented her round face well; the bangs brought out her cheekbones, and the way the edges wisped across her ears hid some of the baby fat on her face. She looked grown-up, like someone who was definitely not afraid of her mother.

She grabbed her purse and jerked open the car door. As she stepped out, she glanced at the contents in her bag: her wallet, the picture she showed her hairdresser, and that tantalizing gold ring glinting up from the bottom of the bag like a challenge. She felt sick; her eyes couldn't break away from the thing. She wondered how she'd ever wear it proudly if she felt this nervous showing her mother a haircut.

She opened the door to the familiar scent of lemon-scented dust cleaner. She should be used to it by now, but it never got less smothering.

Wait. Mom was using a lemon-scented dust cleaner. And yes, the cold salmon tile under her feet was freshly mopped, the green shag carpet had new, crisp vacuum tracks, and the white countertops in the kitchen were recently wiped clean. Mom only cleaned when she was upset. In her panic, Deborah hadn't had time to consider why her mother was home from visiting Gran so early. What happened in Florida? Deborah winced; if Mom was already mad, her hair would only make things worse. Things were bad before they began.

"Debby?" Deborah cringed at the nickname. It made her feel younger and meeker than she wanted to be.

"Is that you?" Her mother's sweet, perky voice called out again from around the corner. She must have been by the sink in the kitchen.

"Yes ma'am," Deborah called back. God, it felt like her heart was in her throat, threatening to spill out along with her words.

She followed the voice, and she was strangely aware of how she was walking; it was all wrong, her center of gravity felt off, and she kept tripping over her own feet. All those hours of practice for the catwalk, and this was the best she could do?

"Good!" Her mother's voice was laced with fake enthusiasm; it was that voice she used to hide how tired she was.

"You're back early," Deborah said. "Is Gran alright?"

"Gran's fine. The surgery went well. She didn't need me for too long."

If there was one thing Deborah's mother taught her without realizing, it was how to pick up on the slightest changes of tone that betrayed frustration, or impatience, or the beginnings of anger. Deborah's tone detector was on high alert today; was that a hint of bitterness in her mother's voice? What happened with Gran? Could Deborah hide her hair long enough for her mother to be in a better mood?

Maybe she could wait until her father got home; she was a daddy's girl after all, all tomboy before her mother whipped her into pageant-shape. Deborah would have appreciated the support. She could use a sibling right now too: a rebellious younger brother of some sort to sand away at her parents' strict edges. Being the only child of a pastor meant she was the subject of her parents' watchful eyes and high expectations at all times. Shame, her constant companion, twinged in her stomach. She couldn't articulate why, but she knew that this haircut would let them down.

Before Deborah could sneak upstairs, her mother called out, "Help me unload the dishwasher, will you?"

"Alright." She would be getting this over with, then.

Deborah was about to turn the corner when she thought it might be best to give her mother some warning. Her fingers fidgeted with the strap of her purse. "So, Mom, I did something this morning."

The plates rattled as Deborah's mother lifted them up from the dishwasher. "You did?"

"Yes ma'am. You know how... how my split ends have been getting worse?"

"Oh yes. They looked atrocious. I fully believe that's the reason you didn't take the crown in Miss Teen Bee."

The comment would have punctured deeper if Deborah wasn't so preoccupied with the present crisis.

"I think you're right. So, I did something about it."

"Please don't tell me you cut it yourself."

"Oh, no ma'am, I went to Tracy."

"I would have liked to have gone with you like we always do, but I guess you're growing up." Her voice took on that helpless tone that made guilt eat at Deborah's edges. Woe to her poor, lonely mother, who was being pushed out of her daughter's life like she was never there. If Deborah was feeling guilty now, it would swallow her whole when she turned the corner.

"Well?" her mother said impatiently. "Are you going to let me see it?"

If Deborah could convert her nerves to electricity, they would power the whole block. Maybe the scientists should work on getting that sorted out instead of messing with the moon.

She plastered on a fake pageant smile. She had acted poised and confident when she had been filled with fear, exhaustion, and self-loathing. This was nothing. This was another show. She steeled herself for her grand entrance. *And from Villa Rica, Georgia, making her way to the gallows, Miss Deborah Mills!*

Deborah turned the corner. Her mother was leaning over the dishwasher, picking up a casserole dish with manicured fingers, her brittle flipped bob bouncing with the movement. She almost dropped the dish when she turned around and saw Deborah's hair.

To her mother's credit, she kept her composure. Smoke didn't billow from her nostrils and she didn't grow any horns. Her tiny mouth, which was descending into a rapid frown, jerked itself into a neutral smile. However, she could not control her thin eyebrows; they shot up her forehead and stayed there.

All that escaped her lips was a dumbfounded, "ah."

Deborah's smile started to crack. "So? What do you think?"

Her mother took just a beat too long to respond. "Oh, honey."

She made her way to the wall phone.

"What are you doing?"

"Getting you a refund, darling." Her voice was still sweet, but it took on a vicious edge. Her fingers pounded the rotary. "Tracy has done so well with your hair until now, I can't *believe*—"

"No, please don't—Mom, I asked for it."

"Don't be ridiculous, hon. I know you hate confrontation, but you've got to—"

"I showed her a picture and everything."

Her mother's steel gaze cut to Deborah's purse. "What picture did you show her?"

Deborah pulled out a crumbled magazine cutting of Mia Farrow. It was a behind-the-scenes shot during the filming of *Rosemary's Baby*, which her mother had not allowed her to see. Deborah's hands shook as she handed the clipping to her mother.

Her mother's eyes narrowed as she scrutinized the picture. "You showed Tracy this?"

"Yes ma'am."

Her mother abandoned the phone. Deborah's radar frantically searched for the slightest twitch of her mouth, the squinting of her eyes, anything that would betray what she was feeling. But her mother was a trained pageant queen, far more trained than Deborah. Her facade did not crack.

What felt like centuries full of tension later, her mother's head began moving in a slow nod. "It's very short."

"Yes ma'am."

"You'll have to explain this to your father."

"Yes ma'am." Deborah felt like a Chatty Cathy doll, repeating the same thing over and over again.

"...It's salvageable, though," her mother said nonchalantly. "It's sassy."

Just the slightest twinge of hope flickered in Deborah's chest. "That's what I thought, too."

"It just needs some curling, that's all."

Deborah did not want it curled. "Oh, I don't know if we have time—"

"Nonsense, Debby. You finish unloading the dishes, and I'll go upstairs and plug in the iron."

Before Deborah could object, her mother placed the casserole dish in her hands and skirted out of the kitchen.

She tried to take a long time with the dishes, she really did. But no matter how many times Deborah pretended to mix up the cabinets or rearrange the silverware, she would have to go upstairs sooner or later. Why couldn't she just tell her mother that she didn't want her hair curled? Her mother took her haircut well enough, what kept Deborah from disagreeing about something as small as a curling iron? For whatever reason, upsetting her mother felt like a horrible, awful thing. It gave way to some primal fear, something that was hard-wired into her brain stem for survival. Maybe it was something evolutionary; scientifically, it made sense for her to freeze up before biting the hand that nursed her, raised her, and sacrificed for her. Yes, it had to be.

But as Deborah dried off the last Tupperware dish, she knew evolutionary excuses were only hiding the truth. She knew the center of it all was that saying *no* prompts the question *why? Why don't you want to curl your hair, why don't you want to do pageants anymore, why do you feel like yourself with your hair short, why don't you date like other girls your age do?* If those were the inevitable questions to be asked, Deborah would make sure her mother would never ask them, because she could not bear to reveal the answers.

She trudged her way up the stairs, passing the sterile family portraits hanging on the eggshell walls. When she got to the top, she leaned her weight against the bathroom door and put on her pageant mask once more.

"Ah, finally," her mother said, patting the pink ottoman in front of the stark-white vanity. The curling iron was already in her hand. "Sit down, Debby."

The nickname chipped away at her already disappearing resolve. The bravado she felt on the drive home felt like a cruel joke, the way it was dissolving into timid obedience. She sat at the ottoman. Deborah and her mother's faces in the mirror looked like an echo: same eyes, same mouth, same cheeks. One face was more worn and tired, but Deborah couldn't tell which one.

Her mother took a longer strand from the center of her head and twisted it around the iron. It barely wrapped around the barrel once. She held it for one, two, three, and the hair fell not in a ringlet, but in a perfect circle. If her mother continued like this, Deborah's head might look like corn on the cob, or like bubble-wrap. But she continued, and Deborah guessed that her mother was determined to wrestle her foreign hair into a shape she liked.

The curling iron was dangerously close to burning her ear. Deborah wondered if Eve ever did her daughter's hair. Then she wondered why she never heard about Eve's daughter. She knew Eve had to have had one if humankind was to last. She wondered what their relationship was like. Maybe it was so complicated, even God couldn't put it into words, and that's why it didn't make it into the Bible. Maybe that was part of the curse Deborah's father preached about this past Sunday; when Eve ate the fruit for wanting to know as much as God did, God made sure all mothers would never be able to know their children, not really. They'd only be able to see them through their own pain and mistakes, and fruitlessly warn their children against flirting with the forbidden.

Deborah realized that the silence between them had stretched for too long. "When's dad coming home?"

Her mother released another tuft of hair from the iron. "When he's finished with his sermon."

"What's it about this week?"

"Sodom and Gomorrah."

"Ah."

A heavy dread rested on Deborah's shoulders. She wished she hadn't asked about the sermon at all; it would have been easier to hide her shame from the front pews and bear it in one fell swoop, but now every mention of Sunday was a reminder of what was to come. She hated those sermons, where she felt dirty and rotten and wrong just for being. She hated even more that she could not leave when she felt the licks of fire at her feet from her father's brimstone preaching, because she was a fixed decoration in the church, just as solid and immovable as the pulpit or the stained glass. The ring in her purse called out to her from the kitchen counter where she had laid it, mocking her cowardice. She was no Saint. She was an impostor.

Deborah didn't want to think about that anymore. "How was your visit to Gran?"

Her mother always looked tired when talking about Gran. "Oh, you know. It was alright. Her knee is healing up nicely. She wishes she could see you more."

"What did you two talk about?"

"About life. Pageants. Church." Her tone was clipped, leaving no room for further questioning.

The heat from the curling iron was making the back of Deborah's neck itch. Her mother kept biting her lip in concentration, trying to get Deborah's hair to curl. It wasn't working. Her mother was getting more irritated by the minute, Deborah could feel it. The iron inched closer and closer to her head, singeing her scalp, painting the tops of her ears red.

Deborah's mother jerked the iron down a stubborn piece of hair in frustration. The iron slipped past the strand and landed on Deborah's neck, white-hot and scalding. She yelped and jumped forward, hands flying to the burn.

"Oh, Debby! I'm so sorry!"

"It's okay."

"No," her mother said, shaking her head. She looked like she just realized something. "It's not okay."

"I'll be fine—"

"How could you go and do this?"

Deborah blinked, confused. "What?"

She looked through the mirror and saw that her mother was not concerned, but angry. Panic flickered anew in her chest.

"How could you ruin your hair like this?" Her mother was near shouting, her thin eyebrows curved upward in a plea. "I can't do anything with it. And when I try, I burn you. Look at yourself!"

Deborah guessed right earlier about bubble wrap. Her hair looked like Gran's when it was in rollers, only there were no rollers keeping it in place; it was so short, it stayed in those tight loops. She couldn't help it, she laughed at the sight. She looked ridiculous.

"This isn't funny!" Her mother insisted. "How are you going to compete with hair like that?"

This was it. They would finally get to the heart of the matter. She still feared letting her mother down, but she was so tired of faking it, of putting on a smile that was just as forced into shape as her hair. She knew she would have to get the words out now before they were stuck in her throat forever.

"Maybe we take a break from competing until it grows back."

Her mother's eyebrows furrowed. "A break? You'll lose your momentum!"

Deborah's laughter picked back up. "What momentum did I have, Momma? I'll just get runner-up again."

"That's because you don't try. If you only put your heart into it, if you really cared, you'd do well. And now you've gone and ruined it. Look at you: you're laughing. You've thrown away your beauty and you're laughing. I hope you enjoy…" her mother scrambled for the right insult. "You enjoy being Miss Helmet-Head!"

Deborah's side was beginning to hurt from all her laughter. Miss Helmet-Head. The irony was that the name didn't hurt like her mother intended. It was a silly Christening of sorts. She wanted nothing more than to be Miss Helmet-Head: bold enough to be strange, confident enough to be unpolished, containing enough love and acceptance for herself that she'd be fine if she were unloved by others.

"Deborah May, you stop it right now!"

The mention of her middle name turned her lungs into a vacuum. All the laughter was sucked out in an instant, replaced by that same primal fear she felt at the dishwasher.

"This isn't funny," her mother snapped. "This is serious. You are playing a dangerous game, young lady. You're not Mia Farrow, you're a Mills, and a Mills carries themselves with more dignity than chopping off their hair on a whim—"

"It wasn't a whim—"

"Don't you dare interrupt me! People expect things from us, Debby, and it's not this. When you act a fool, you don't just hurt your name, you hurt your father's. You know this, Debby."

Deborah was too ashamed to reply. She shook her head in solemn agreement and wiped the snot escaping from her nose.

Her mother wasn't done. "My Lord, Debby. What were you thinking? Please tell me, Debby. I want to know."

Each "Debby" felt like a blow, reminding her how small and awful she was. *People expect things from us*, Debby, *you know this* Debby, *please tell me*, Debby.

The held-in sobs built up pressure in her throat that made her voice come out in a croak. "I don't want to just take a break. I... I don't want to do pageants anymore."

The look of admonishment on her mother's face vanished, and her voice became soothing. "Oh, hon."

The dam broke. Sobs that were months in the making burst through at once. She felt her mother's arms around her, and Deborah pressed her face into her shoulder. Her eyes caught her ridiculous, helmet-head, tear-soaked reflection in the mirror, and an unhinged laugh escaped her lips. *The impostor shows her true colors.*

Her mother said in her ear, "I don't understand. You love pageants."

"I do. But... I don't like the me that does pageants."

The arms around Deborah tensed; she could tell that her words had confused her. She elaborated, "I don't like pretending I'm something I'm not."

Her mother laughed, not in a teasing, harsh way, but in a way that suggested relief. "Oh, honey. That's what you do in pageants. It's a life skill. It's why I got you involved in them so young. And now, everyone tells me how mature and lovely you are. My mother did the same for me, and it did me good."

But at what cost? Deborah's mother hated seeing Gran. At Thanksgivings and Christmases, all Deborah could notice was how Gran criticized every little thing her mother did—her posture, the plate settings, her weight—and now, not even surgery could keep Gran's daughter at her side. Was Deborah's relationship with her mother fated for that, too?

"Why did you leave Florida early?"

"Don't try to change the subject—"

"What did she say?"

Her mother huffed. "If I tell you, will you give me a straight answer to anything I ask?"

It was a dangerous bargain, but Deborah nodded anyway.

"She said... well, it wasn't just one thing. It was like she always is. They were little things, one every second. I couldn't take it for two more days, I just had to get out of there. Now, Deborah." She placed her hands on Deborah's shoulders. "Why did you cut your hair?"

Deborah thought of the joy she had felt on the drive home. She thought of how all the feminine things her mother enjoyed were to her like Saul's armor. She thought of how her friends' first kisses with boys had felt like fireworks and magic, and her first kiss had felt like nothing at all. She thought of *The Ladder* periodical that a classmate had let her borrow with a wink, the pages filled with interviews with women who wore pinky rings like the one at the bottom of her purse. She thought of all the nights she begged God to change her, and no matter how hard she cried, he never answered.

Deborah pulled back to look her mother in the face. "I think... I think I'm different—"

"No, you're not."

"But I—"

"You don't want to be. You may think this... this new style is cool, but it's not worth it. People treat you different when you're different, Deborah.

Trust me on this." Her mother's tight lips started wobbling. An old memory tugged on Deborah's attention; it was one of her mother's rare stories of her childhood. What was the word she had used to describe her eight year old self? "Fluffy," she had said. "I was a fluffy thing, and the other girls knew it. My mom had me on diets by third grade." Deborah's mother had laughed it off then. She wasn't laughing now.

Something thawed in Deborah's chest. The world must have been a scary place for a girl who was taught to hate herself so young. In her mother's smothering way, she was trying to protect her. She showed Deborah from the beginning how to self-dilute for survival, for acceptance, for love. Her mother wasn't angry, evil, or controlling. She was afraid.

"I know," Deborah said, wiping her face. "But I think I need to see if it's worth it."

Her mother sighed, and in her eyes, Deborah could see a disappointment that was reserved for parents who knew that things could only go wrong, and that none of their words could stop it.

"I think so too. But in your trying, remember—"

"Yes ma'am, I'm a Mills." Despite it all, the mantle still remained.

Her mother ran her fingers through Deborah's hair. "It needs to be brushed out."

As her mother teased her hair, they discussed what she could do this summer instead of pageantry. She could go to church camp, something she had missed out on in the past with pageant training. She mentioned working at the movie theater, and her mother agreed only if she didn't watch any of the movies. Summer, in the span of an hour, had transformed from drudgery to possibility.

The next day, as she was leaving to go to the theater for a job application, she found her purse on the kitchen counter from the day before. The ring was still there, only it didn't mock. It seemed to whisper, *are you ready?*

Not entirely. But today, she could begin.

As she got in the car, she slipped the ring over her right pinky. It made a pleasant clicking noise as she tapped the beat of the radio to her steering wheel. She rolled the window down and let the late Spring breeze brush its way through her new hair, her crown, her helmet-head.

My Family Reunion

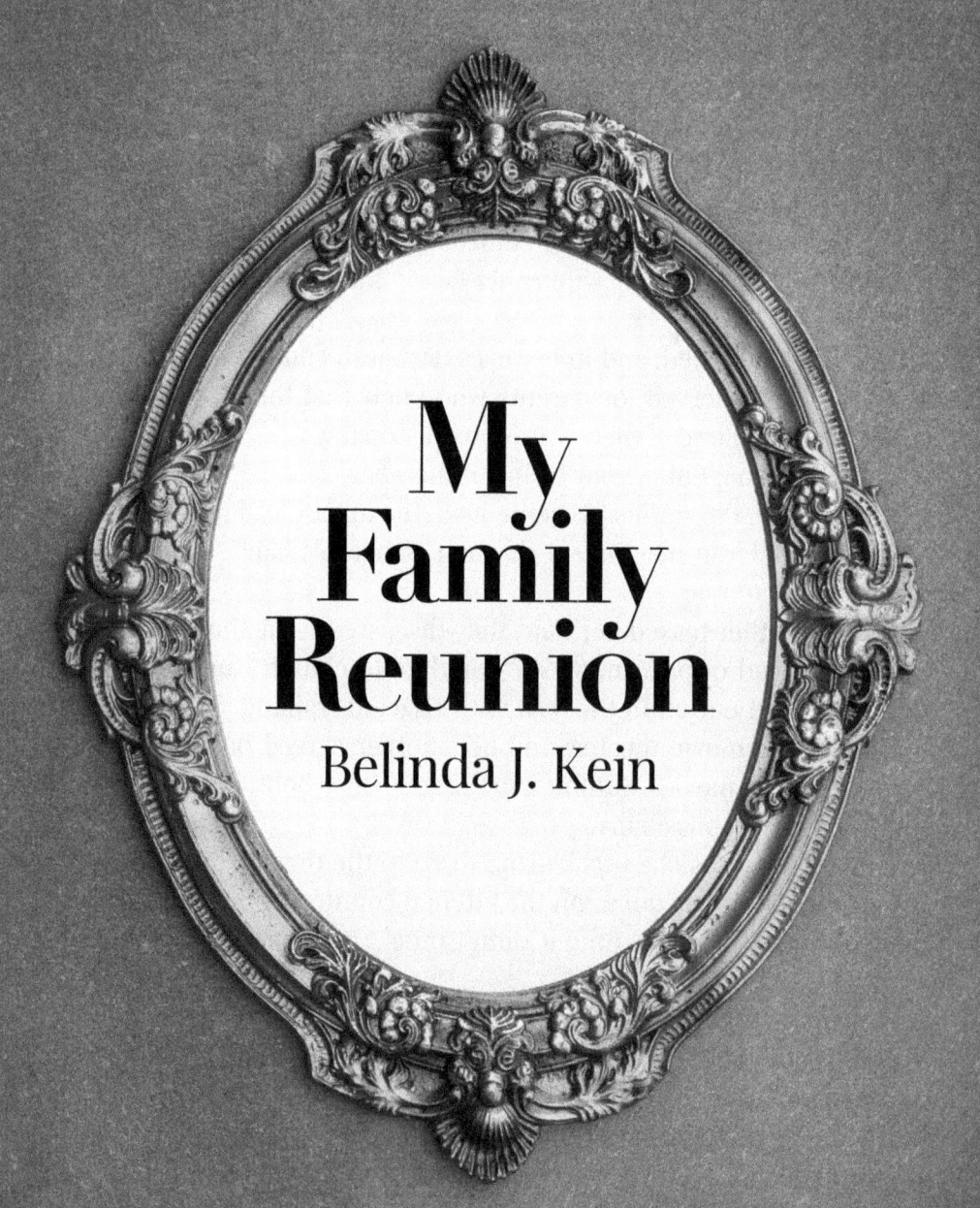

Belinda J. Kein

[NONFICTION]

It's undeniable that I have aged. The years have had their way with me. They've left me shrunk and shriveled, turned my wavy mane slack and thin, threaded it with strands of silver. It's gone snow-white at my temples, the way my father's did. I see him in my own face in the mirror, the man he was before the cancer. Before the dire prognosis. Before it ravaged him. He shed not a tear, allowed himself not one moment of self-pity. It wasn't stoicism. It was an adamant refusal to let go his hold on life. His deep, robust, resonant laugh told you so. He laughed loudest at his own jokes. And he remained a resolute jokester throughout the ordeal.

He outlived every expectation, through fall and winter, spring in all its verdant glory. When Passover arrived, he was barely skin and bone.

No longer ambulatory, he'd been relegated to the bedroom. Exiled might be the better word. The rest of us were in the living room. We'd gathered around a long folding table shrouded in a tablecloth for the occasion. A place was set for Elijah. Matzo was piled high. We were well into retelling the story of the Israelites' escape from Egypt, forty years of wandering the Sinai desert. We were also well into a bottle of Manischewitz, crazed with hunger and more than a little bored.

My mother, known to burst into song at the slightest provocation and for her inability to carry a tune, took it upon herself to remedy our ennui. With gusto and volume enough to shout down our objections, she launched into a screeching rendition of "Climb Every Mountain." It was not lost on us. We had all seen the movie *The Sound of Music*. My father had dragged us to the theater to watch it with him on numerous occasions. At one time, he could play every song on his accordion and did so frequently, much to our chagrin. Though my mother was Jewish, as were my sisters and I by default, my father was not. He was born in Germany and had vehemently opposed, and barely escaped induction into, Hitler's murderous army.

Now diminished as he was, my mother's discordant song was enough to rouse him. It must have required all his remaining strength to send his words up from the bedroom in mocking protest. "I'm not dead yet!" he cried. "But, if I was, with all that damned racket, you would've woke me up!"

Hours later, he was gone. Those would be his parting words oft repeated by my mother, eyes moist, lips quivering with inappropriate glee. Her listeners likely thought her irreverent. But I'm certain, had my father heard her, he would have laughed loud and long. Many years gone now herself, I see her in my countenance, too. In the gray-green gaze we shared, the fading roses in my rotund cheeks, the pronounced pout I inherited late in life, her disappointment made manifest in me.

Now and again, when I glance into a mirror, my sisters will reveal themselves through me as well. My every expression and gesture brings them to the forefront. That I am able to conjure them in this way feels miraculous. It's as if the years in passing have eroded our differences, leaving clearly discernible our similarities. We spent a lifetime laying claim to our distinctions. Yet, for all our efforts to individuate by way of style, demeanor, and general propensity, it appears we're very much alike, after all. I cannot help but grin at the thought. They grin back at me, my own features showing their pleasure. It feels like a reunion, without the family fracas.

[POETRY]

Museologies

By: Rebecca Pyle

Never tell a muse they are a muse. Never tell anyone you have
A muse. It is the worst of news to those who wish they had one and
Will never find one: muses only happen when you do not try. To tell a
Muse they are your muse is to tell them they are a phantasm, not appealing
To most people. It's best to say you're inspired by stones or boulders or Indians,
Better to pretend spirits gather around you who've protected you since infancy, and
None have names. I like an array of lilies, blue earthenware plates, and chocolates, but
The lilies will wilt and turn the water dirty, the plates will need washing and shining,
And chocolates are always eaten and forgotten. Not like muses, who keep up a drum
Fire of declensions and perimeter and valiance, and never die. There is no death for
Muses: they have the fire of early-childhood friends, who only see good about you
No matter what you do. I'd rather not go swimming in the ocean, as I'm old; but
A muse is there, swimming for you, bringing back what he or she learns from
The sea and the westerlies. All your shoes are their favorites. So are your
Ways of walking down the beach, avoiding locals, and your way of
Falling asleep in the afternoon, dodging social obligations. Yes,
Muses say, you are friendless, and best that way: tell my story
Till the beach ends, till fossil fuel cars go cold and used
And gone.

Jersey Devil
Kelsey Myers

[FICTION]

Chuck had ten pages on Homer due after the long weekend was over. Twenty pages, if you counted the fact that Charles "Chuck" Barnham, as one of St. Joseph's Academy for Boys's pitiful scholarship students, had been roped into doing Vincent Montague's homework sometime last year in exchange for the pleasure of hanging with Montague's gang. A deal that had its benefits, he had thought at the time, and its drawbacks, but since Montague normally didn't bother to talk to him except to say things like "watch out, Barnham, I'm coming through," and since the rest of the student body didn't seem particularly inclined to talk to him either, Chuck figured he should take his friends where he could get them, even if it meant a little extra work.

The arrangement had begun last spring, in their

Photography: Dhilip Antony

sophomore year, 1916. "We'll take you out for a trial run," Montague said with good humor. When Chuck called him "Vincent," a few weeks later, he insisted on being called "Monty."

"We're friends now, aren't we, Chucky?" Monty asked, with that easy, lazy grin that made the corners of his eyes crinkle. Chuck would've liked to think he wasn't so desperate that he'd believe it, but he did, God help him. A rich boy was using him for his school smarts and suddenly he's all smitten just because someone's paying him the least bit of attention.

The next year, Monty, Chuck, and the other two members of the game moved into a four-bed room in the junior boys' dormitory. It was a better fit than his last dorm mates, who'd snored and crumpled up his essays and generally just been upper-class pricks, but Chuck still wasn't certain he fit into this space, with these people, despite the fact that Monty kept insisting they were friends.

Whether they were friends or not, Chuck was still writing all his literature essays. It was important, for the sake of not getting caught, not just to write two good papers but to write two different papers on different subjects. Chuck was a thorough plagiarist, it turned out. He'd asked Monty for copies of his old papers, the ones that were getting failing grades. The professor would get suspicious if Monty's abilities sky-rocketed or if his vocabulary suddenly shifted, so Chuck made gradual improvements, mimicking Monty's style. It worked, Monty was pleased as ever, and Chuck got to stay his friend.

When Monty came in that day, Chuck was working on the Homer essays, the rest of the group was scattered around the dorm room, the sunset flooding the space with purple and orange hues. James was lying flat on his back, legs spread out on his bed, trying to read a copy of *The Iliad*. Chuck had seen him like this before. James was sharp, wouldn't have needed to ask a scholarship boy to do his homework, but he got distracted sometimes. Probably waiting for Monty to get back.

Mousy, meanwhile, named for his narrow shoulders and wide eyes and tendency to twitch, was sitting at his desk, reading some novel that was totally unrelated to the Homer assignment. Mousy was of the opinion that there was no use in doing schoolwork anymore, with the war waging. Chuck knew he'd probably turn in some too-short essay he hadn't even tried to make coherent, probably without reading the book.

Monty clapped his hand on James's knee as he passed, causing the other boy to sit up, before easing over to Chuck's desk and affectionately ruffling his hair. "What'd you land on, Chucky?"

Monty made a show out of everything; it was one of the things Chuck liked most about him, that certain flair for the dramatic. He liked it in Monty because he knew he could never pull it off himself. Sometimes Monty clapped him on the shoulder and said, "you know, old boy—" and Chuck wouldn't even be able to listen to the rest of the sentence, so thrown by the language and so convinced that he'd never be able to pull off the same.

"The role of the gods in the ending of the Trojan war?" Monty asked, a teasing note in his rich voice, which always sounded like he was about to chuckle. "The recurring theme of wrath? Homeric honor, you know, that great big manly honor?"

Chuck reached up to try and put his hair back into place. Monty was still peering over his shoulder. "I don't know why you don't do this work yourself if you know so much about it."

"We all know Monty can't write worth a damn," James said, folding his knees in front of him. James could be jovial sometimes, but he must be in some kind of mood today, because his tone was bitter. "Besides, if he spent all day writing papers, he wouldn't have time for all the drinking and debauchery, isn't that right, Monty?"

Chuck could never quite tell if James and Monty were friends or enemies, even though they claimed to be best friends. Sometimes they sniped back and forth at each other like rivals; other times Chuck would see James lean his head on Monty's shoulder, which had to be awkward, because Monty was quite a bit taller. His personal theory, which he would never breathe aloud, was that James didn't like sharing his best friend.

"Speaking of which." Monty reached into his school bag and pulled out a sizable bottle of scotch in a clear glass decanter, filled right about up to the top. A mite bit finer than the cheap stuff some of the older boys shared with them from flasks for a price.

"C'mon, Chucky," Monty said, "tell us what you're working on and I'll give you a little taste."

"Where in God's name did you get that?"

"I asked you first."

Christ. In moments like these, Chuck was sure that Vincent Montague was going to be the death of him. He closed his copy of *The Iliad* and turned around in his chair, eying the decanter warily—but not without interest.

He'd almost forgotten Mousy was there—that happened a lot—but they made eye contact as he turned in his chair. The smaller boy's face was unreadable. He usually turned down the flasks when the older boys offered them. Chuck was never sure where he stood with Mousy. He was pretty sure they were friends. Mouse had never said anything to the contrary. Nothing in the affirmative, either. Mouse didn't say much. He and Monty were friends from way back. Monty told Chuck once that Mouse used to be more "sociable." "I don't give up on a friend," Monty said at the time.

Even one you only keep around because he does your homework?

"The subject?" Monty prompted.

Right. "I'm writing about honor," Chuck said dryly—they'd been doing this long enough that when Monty pushed him, Chuck could push back. Actually, Monty seemed to prefer it that way. "You're writing about Achilles and Patroclus."

"Oh, and what is he studying next, Oscar Wilde?" The insinuation was a nasty one, but Chuck didn't have the clout here to glare. It was an all boys' school. That sort of thing happened, now and again. Expulsions had resulted in the past, but most of the lads here were clever enough not to get caught. It didn't mean anything, it was just because there weren't any girls around. Chuck had thought about going for it once or twice, but who would he ask? How would he ask? The logistics seemed confusing.

It turned out that Chuck didn't have to glare, because Monty did it for him. "You're in fine spirits tonight, James."

"Just how you like me, Monty," James grumbled. But he perked up a bit at the attention, and sprang from the bed, reaching for the decanter.

"Where'd you get the scotch, Monty?" Mousy asked. It was the first time he'd spoken in hours.

"Oh, you," Monty whined. He uncapped the decanter and took a brief swig before James could get his hands on it, elbowing the other boy away. "You're just going to chastise me."

"Only if you've done something worth chastising for."

"Alright, *father*." James was still reaching for the bottle; Monty pressed it into his hands and pushed him back onto his bed. James took a swig, crawling up to the head of the bed, while Monty sat at the foot, cross-legged. "I stole it from the dean's office, are you offended?"

A pause as Mousy considered. "Alright," he said. "Give it here."

Chuck would've expected a no, but Monty did have a certain way of influencing people. Or maybe Mouse just turned down all that cheap scotch because it was cheap. Chuck knew they were too young to have an appreciation for fine scotch, but if this came from the dean's office, this was fine scotch, and that was something to be cherished.

"Not a lot of scotch that fine where you're planning on going, Mousy," James said. The bite was gone from his voice, but there was danger in his lazy tone. "Just rationed cigarettes and piss-weak coffee in a tin cup."

Even Chuck cringed. "Not this again," Monty groaned. He leaned back on the bed, curly black hair resting on James's curled legs. That kind of touching was limited to James and Monty, unless you counted Monty ruffling Chuck's hair. "You get Mousy started on the war and he won't stop."

"It'll all be over before we graduate, anyway," James said, sitting up and reaching for the decanter so that he could have a swig. Chuck was still in his desk chair, watching all of this unfold. He wasn't sure that was true, that the war would be over in time. He tried not to think about it very much, because when he thought about going to Europe to fight he got this sick feeling of dread in his stomach, like heavy gray clouds about to start storming.

"But Mousy wants to go now," Monty said. "Isn't that right, Mousy?"

"They'll take eighteen-year-olds if you lie about your age," Mousy said, in the voice of someone who had said such a thing a thousand times. This was not the first time the gang had had this argument.

"But why would you want to?" Chuck normally didn't interrupt the others while they were riffing, but this riffing had serious connotations, and he was fond of Mousy. Mousy with the mousy-brown hair, who had never been in a fist fight before, let alone fired a gun. That sick feeling he got when he thought about going over to Europe—he got the same sick feeling when he imagined Mousy doing the same.

"For King and Country, of course," James drawled in a British accent. "Here, Chucky, have some of this."

Chuck hesitated. "I should finish these essays, I don't know if I want to…"

"Barnham, you don't have a history of robbing your father's well stocked and very expensive liquor cabinet," James said. "This is very good scotch."

He always felt awkward around James; the other boy had never said outright that he didn't like him, but there were ways of telling. Chuck noticed things, the same way he noticed that Monty and James were touchy, or that James didn't like other people around Monty. There was something venomous in James's tone when he talked to Chuck, always had been, and Chuck didn't have the first clue what he'd done to deserve it.

So he walked past Monty on the edge of the bed and took the decanter.

Sniffed the scotch inside, to James's derisive laughter, and took a swig. It took everything in him not to cough it up. He just didn't drink that much and, even if it was fine, this stuff burned.

"Of course the scholarship boy doesn't know how to drink," James scoffed.

Monty slapped his thigh, hard. "Be nice."

"Have some more, Chuck," James said. "Go on. A big one this time."

His mouth was still on fire from the last sip, but he wasn't about to refuse James. The truth was that as smart as he was, he didn't have the power here. Beyond wanting to be Monty's friend, these boys had fathers who were titans of industry. He had to think about weaseling his way into a job after prep school and college, after all.

So he took a big gulp of the scotch, nearly spit it all over the dorm room but managed to swallow it down. There were tears in his eyes as he bent over, convinced he was about to vomit all that very fine scotch up on the dorm room carpet. He swallowed down a bit of his own bile, straightened, and exhaled sharply, trying to breathe.

"There's a lad," James said. "Don't you want one more?"

"That's enough." Monty's tone was stricter than usual, icy; he got up from James's bed, snatched the scotch away from Chuck, who was still breathing heavy, and placed an arm around Chuck's shoulders. "Besides," he said, looking at James. "I just had a brilliant idea."

Monty's brilliant ideas usually ended in disaster, leading to detention and to Chuck writing letters home to his parents explaining how he'd just got caught up in the spirit of things, that was all. *I expect better from you*, his father had said in response, every time.

"Oh?" James drawled. If he was put out that his game was put on hold, he didn't show it.

"I'll stay here and finish your essay, right?" Chuck stumbled a bit back to his desk, reaching for his fountain pen. Monty reached out and stopped his arm.

"We're better friends than that, don't you think?" he said. Every time Monty called him his friend, his heart just blossomed. But there was underlying desperation in that blooming feeling. He shouldn't care so much.

"You can do it hungover tomorrow," Monty said. "Grab your coat and bundle up, Chucky. We're going into the Pine Barrens."

Mousy groaned. "Why," he asked, "why, why are we going into the Pine Barrens?"

The Pine Barrens stretched between south New Jersey and Pennsylvania, a great and mostly untouched stretch of forest and wildlife. St. Joseph's was right on the edge, and every so often, the boys would go out into the forest to smoke or drink. It was risky territory at night, even with a lantern, because none of the boys in that academy really knew what lurked in those woods, and they whispered, sometimes, about dark things.

"Just a little stretch of it," Monty said in the tone of a protest, as if offended that Mousy would question his idea. "To get to the Catholic all-girls school on the other side." Chuck didn't have to look at James to know the anger that one sentence would inspire. In fact, he was very purposefully avoiding looking at James, lest he become the subject of the other boy's ire.

Chuck knew better than this, but that was how it always went. Monty came up with some ridiculous, hare-brained idea, and Chuck would know that he should say no and stay in and work on homework, but he would wind up joining the boys for the adventure and then they'd all get detention. And then he'd have to write to his mother and father.

Still, habits were hard to break. "I'm in," he said.

Monty grinned and clapped him on the back. "There we go," he said. "The rest of you sons of bitches coming?"

"If you two go into that forest alone you're going to be mauled by a bear," James said, grumbling again. He went to the coat closet, looking for his sturdiest boots. "Mouse?"

Mousy usually stayed out of these things. He blinked slowly, as though he were a cat. "You're all going to die," he said. "The *Pine Barrens*."

"Just a little stretch," Monty corrected.

"So come and die with us," James said, properly and warmly dressed. "C'mon, Mouse, come and have some fun before they ship you overseas."

"I'm not carrying your corpses back to the school," Mousy said, but to Monty's absolute joy, he went and fetched his coat.

It was Saturday night, dusk, on President's Day weekend, and the grounds of St. Joseph's were curiously bare as the boys traveled out the main doors of the dormitory and snuck around back to the forest not so far away. No snow on the ground, but the kind of frost that crunched beneath their boots, as if they were breaking blades of grass every time they made a step. A bad thing, if they did run into a bear and wanted to hide and keep quiet, and who knew what lurked in the Pine Barrens? Could be bears. But apart from Mousy, who'd only had that first swig, everyone was drunk enough not to worry about it.

James and Monty were keeping their distance from each other—Monty leading the way with his lantern, a box of matches in his knapsack—except to pass the decanter back and forth. They were drinking most of it; Chuck had decided that if he was going to develop a taste for scotch, it wasn't going to be while he was sixteen years old and at prep school. The other two boys weren't holding back, though, and had made an impressive dent in the bottle by the time they'd crossed the threshold of the forest. Monty was tall like a tree, seemed to bend like a willow in the wind, unsteady on his feet. After a while, James, a little more sober, reached to stretch an arm around his shoulders to keep him steady. For a second, Chuck thought they'd made up, until—

"So what are you going to do with those Catholic girls, anyway, Monty?"

Monty said nothing, but James kept talking.

"Hear their legs are held together tighter than a vice," James continued. His voice was a half-whisper, and Chuck knew he shouldn't be listening; he listened anyway, straining his ears to hear. "And that's if we don't get caught by the nuns who watch them, unless you're intending on having your way with the Mother Superior, too? Would you even know what to do with a girl once her legs—"

Monty shoved him, hard, and James stumbled, knocking into a tree with a curse. "Don't touch me," he said. "I can walk by myself."

In the dim light of the lantern, James looked ready to protest, but some wisdom deep inside his brain must've told him better, because he kept his mouth shut. For a second, just a second, before he fell back between Chuck and Mousy and dug an elbow into Mousy's ribs.

"This where you wanna be, Mouse? German forests with a rifle in your arms?"

Mousy said nothing back. He'd said nothing at all since they'd left the dormitory. Chuck glanced over, wondering if he should do something, say something.

"Or would you rather be in the trenches? Bullets whizzing by your head so close they graze the back of your neck, all the dirt and mud and shit? Digging latrines, is that where you want to be? Will that help you serve your country?"

There was a voice inside Chuck's head that told him to let it go. He ignored that voice. "Leave it alone," he said sharply, as sharply as he could, trying to sound as sure as himself as James usually sounded.

It didn't work. "You sure you want to speak to me that way, Barnham?" he snapped. "We all know why you're here, and it's not because you write such excellent essays."

He should back down. Maybe it was the scotch. Maybe it was because he truly didn't know what James was talking about. "Yeah?" he said, trying to keep his voice strong; it wavered anyway. "What am I here for, then?"

"Because Montague needs a pet project," James said. "Or maybe just a pet."

"You want me to hit you with this lantern, James?" Monty said, not looking back behind him. Chuck was pretty sure that was because if Monty tried to look behind him, he would lose his balance and fall over drunk. "How about the decanter? Emptier than it used to be, but pretty heavy, glass, should do some damage."

It certainly didn't calm James down, but it did make him shut up. Chuck took a deep breath, suddenly dizzy, overwhelmed. He wasn't sure if it was the gulps of scotch catching up with him or what James had just insinuated. "Maybe we should turn back," Chuck said. "I'm getting a little—I mean, we didn't bring any water, and I think I at least need to sit down-"

"I told you, scholarship boy can't hold his liquor—"

"Enough, James." Monty turned around very slowly, as though he were waddling. "Alright, we could turn back, we could, but there's a problem there, not an insurmountable problem, but a problem nonetheless, and the problem is this—"

"You're lost," Mousy said. Chuck's stomach sank.

There were no sign posts, no paths, no indicators of where they were, and it wasn't like they'd been dropping bread crumbs since the moment they entered the forest. But they'd walked in a straight line—they should be able to find their way back, Chuck thought, surely. They hadn't gone too far, right?

But night had fallen, and he didn't trust himself to walk. He certainly didn't trust Monty to walk any further. There was a little clearing up ahead; Mousy took Monty's arm, led him there, and the others followed. "Anyone know how to light a campfire?" Mouse asked, the most sober of them all, their hero, the one who would save them.

Dead silence, all around.

"We could still spend the night here," Chuck said, as if he were trying to convince himself. "Sleep on the ground—you've got matches, we can keep the lantern going—and find our way back when the light comes. Back at St.

Joseph's by morning, no one having known we've gone anywhere."

"You want us to spend the night in the Pine Barrens?" Monty set the lantern down, pulled his coat tighter around him.

James chuckled. It was a dark chuckle. "What," he said, "are you afraid of the Jersey Devil?"

Chuck eased himself onto the ground; his legs were going to give out if he didn't. The other boys followed suit, forming a little campfire circle around the lantern. "What's the Jersey Devil?"

"I forget you're from corn country." Now that the prospect of canoodling with Catholic girls was off the table, James seemed calmer. He did that thing again, rested his head on Monty's shoulder; Monty looked as though he might push him off, but he didn't. "You tell the story," he said to Monty. "You are the best at telling stories."

"Don't flatter me, I'll believe it." Monty's limbs seemed to relax for the first time since they'd entered the forest—his forehead was no longer creased. "Alright, I'll tell it."

"Let me take you back 150 years, to a cabin in Southern Jersey and a woman named Mrs. Leeds. Twelve children she'd carried in her womb and twelve children she'd delivered. That has to wear on a woman, don't you think? Us men, we don't have to think about the nasty bits of childbirth. You ever see a child being born?"

He didn't wait for an answer. "My mother went into labor before the doctors could rush her to the hospital, so she was born in my parents' marriage bed. I wasn't supposed to be anywhere near there, but I heard the screaming. And I peeked my head in, and I saw the blood. There's only a limited window of time a woman can have children. So those thirteen children... over how many years, fifteen? That excruciating pain every time."

"Not to mention feeding thirteen mouths, which is something none of us have ever had to worry about," he continued. "So I understand, I do, why when she found out she was pregnant she tore out her hair and cried out in disgust, 'let it be the devil'!"

"Words have power," Monty said. Chuck, drunk as he was, was enraptured. James was closing his eyes, falling asleep to the sound of Monty's voice. Mousy was silent and still. "So the baby arrived, only it wasn't a baby, it was a devil. Gave an ear-shattering screech, unfolded its wings, and flew out the window and into the Pine Barrens, where he lurks to this day."

"What does he do?" Chuck asked, drunk enough to be curious about this.

"Oh, the usual things. Raiding chicken coops, destroying crops. The kind of things country people worry about." Country people meant poor people. "But I hear he's a fearsome sight, the Jersey Devil, and I wouldn't want to be caught alone with him alone in a dark woods at night, those monstrous flapping wings, those beady eyes, those vicious, sharp, teeth. You know what devils do. They wound."

"Horseshit," James mumbled, half way between sleep and waking.

"Don't you drift off yet," Monty said. Out of all of them, he had the best grip on his words when he was smashed. He could deliver eloquent stories or tell detailed tales. Sometimes none of it made sense. But he was coherent. At least until he started slurring his words. "Someone pass the scotch."

"I thought you had it," Chuck said. "Threatening to, you know. Bash James's head in?"

"I took it before he could. Here. It'll keep us warm, at least." Mousy took a swig, grimaced, and handed the decanter to Monty, who took a swig and handed it to James. James held it out to Chuck, and for a second he thought James might say sorry, but when Chuck declined the bottle, James said nothing at all.

"You and me need to have words," Monty murmured to James, but he didn't sound mad.

"Words," James mumbled.

Normally Chuck wouldn't have cared what those words were; he'd turned a blind eye to many, many signs since he'd begun living with James and Monty, and maybe it was deliberate obliviousness, because whatever they had going on seemed deeper and more significant than a kiss in a broom closet because there weren't any girls around. They touched each other, they leaned on each other, they were affectionate with each other. And Chuck wanted to say he didn't really care, except that he seemed to have been roped into this, too. Monty ruffling his hair. Montague's pet. Did other people call him that?

It was the last thing he should be worrying about on a February night in the middle of the forest, but it was the first thing on his mind. So when James and Monty stumbled off a few yards away, he made a shushing motion towards Mousy and tried to crawl closer so he could hear.

"—jealous," Monty was saying. "You don't need to be."

"Cross the Pine Barrens to see girls—"

"Only because you were being an ass."

"Only because you had your hands all over Barnham."

"I touched his hair."

"You like touching people's hair."

"You're drunk."

"So are you. You like touching people's hair. And you like flirting. And you like that dopey little smile he gets when you call yourself his friend. Are you?"

"What?"

"His friend."

"You're not going to lose me," Monty said. He sounded tired. He sounded as though he'd said this or something like it a million times. This wasn't a new argument. They'd gone through these paces before. Probably since Chuck had started writing Monty's essays.

He couldn't say he felt nothing when Monty... doted on him, god, it all sounded so feminine, but that was what it was. And that blooming feeling that happened in his chest, that blossoming of flowers, he'd been trying so hard for so long to insist it didn't mean anything. But when Monty entered the picture, the lines between platonic and—god, did he have to think the words—*romantic* tended to blur. It took hearing James's jealousy for him to realize what had been in his subconscious all along—that what had been going on between them might be closer to flirtation than friendship, the way Monty pushed and Chuck pushed back, the habit Monty had fallen into of ruffling Chuck's hair.

But there was James to consider. James, with his temper, and that sour look on his face every time he looked at Chuck; they were in love, that must be it, and as soon as he thought it Chuck realized he'd known it all along.

It didn't matter. James wasn't going to lose Monty, Monty wasn't going to lose James, and Chuck was the scholarship boy, and no one was ever going to love the scholarship boy. Not that he was even interested in—more.

He crept back to the lantern, where Mousy was drawing in the dirt with some sticks. This meant something else, too, he realized. It meant he had power over James. And he had never had power once in his life.

He could be cruel with that power. He could lean into the flirting, the touching. Play it up, flirt back. Or he could be merciful. Stick to writing Monty's papers and quietly cherish what seemed to be a genuine friendship. But to know he affected the other boy in that way was a tremulous feeling, one he wasn't sure whether or not he liked. He'd never had the chance to break someone's heart before. And James had it coming.

Mousy had been quiet this whole time—whether he was lost in thought, or drifting off into sleep, Chuck couldn't tell. But when Chuck came back to the lantern, Mouse finally spoke up. "You should come back to the light," he called. "Get some rest. Sort it out when you're sober."

The couple managed their way back to the circle. They traded swigs of scotch before lying down in the dirt, James's knees curled up to his chest, Monty lying flat on the back. It wasn't long before both of them were out.

"Not sleepy?" Chuck asked Mouse, who was toying with the sticks in his hands like they were toy soldiers, turning them over and over between his fingers.

"No," he said.

"You look deep in thought."

Mousy dropped the sticks, brought his hands to his cheeks and held his face in his palms. "I have a lot to think about."

"You ever think about anything other than the war?"

"Not really."

"Tell me why."

"You know all the reasons."

"So tell me again."

"I want to serve my country," Mousy said.

"You've said that so many times," Chuck said. Over and over and over again, Mouse had claimed he was doing this to be—what, patriotic? Something was in Chuck tonight, there was magic in the air tonight, or maybe it was alcohol; something was making him bolder. "I don't believe it anymore."

Mouse laughed. Chuck had never seen someone so young look so tired. "You think that's all it takes to get someone to admit to something they don't want to admit to?" he asked. "Pointing out a lie doesn't tell you what the truth is."

"We're not friends," Chuck said, realizing it as he said it aloud.

"No." Mousy didn't say it unkindly, but he said it.

Chuck paused. "You're planning on running away before morning comes."

That caught Mouse's attention. He glanced up, a tiny smile twitching at his lips. "Now, why would you say that?"

"You've been talking about it for ages, and it's the perfect opportunity," Chuck said. "I bet you knew where we were going the entire time, and you didn't correct Monty because you wanted us off course. Bunch of boys go into a forest, one doesn't come out, it happens. They'll say the Jersey Devil got you. You're planning on taking the lantern and running away before morning comes."

Mouse was silent for a while. This was a strike in the dark for Chuck; he wasn't nearly as confident as he sounded. But it made sense to him. All the clues pointed in this direction.

"You gonna stop me?" Mousy asked.

So he was right. The thing to do, it seemed to Chuck, was to try and stop him. He'd die over there. Everyone would die over there; maybe, if the war went on long enough, everyone would die everywhere. He didn't understand why someone would want to be a part of that.

But it wasn't his decision to make, or his life to live, or his death to die.

"No," he said, "but I want you to tell me why."

Mousy chewed on his bottom lip. "I don't want to be my father's son."

"Neither do I. What does that have to do with it?"

Mousy tilted his head. "I never thought about it. That you might have your own burdens. That your father might expect things from you. Mine expects things from me. The military—it's a choice. I could go. Have my own career. My own life. Not his choice. My choice."

"That," Chuck said, "seems like a stupid reason to sign up to die."

"Plenty of people die in war," Mousy said. "Plenty of people don't. I've made my peace with that."

"Mousy," Chuck said, baffled. "You're sixteen. How have you made peace with death?"

"When you don't feel like you're alive, it doesn't make a difference."

Chuck paused again, chewed that over in his mind. He'd felt sad sometimes, sure. Lonely. But feeling like he wasn't alive? That seemed like a gray sky he'd never seen before. "You feel that way?"

"Yeah." Mousy dusted his palms on his knees, got up and took the lantern. "Get some sleep, Chuck. We're not far in, you'll be able to find your way back in the morning."

He could stop him, right now. And in stopping him, he could save his life. That was power, too. Suddenly the thought of that kind of power made him feel sick. Gray fog in his abdomen, lead dread in his stomach.

But it didn't matter. Mousy must've taken his silence for assent, because he saluted, turned, and left.

Chuck lay awake in the dark and thought about leathery wings.

The Jersey Devil had been a baby when he'd been born. A baby devil, but just a baby. Babies needed their mothers, but the Jersey Devil hadn't. He had sprouted from between her parted legs—he must have been covered in her blood—and the first thing he did was screech. That was the first thing any baby did. They cried. Doctors got alarmed if they didn't.

Chuck's younger brother, who was not so lucky as to receive a scholarship to a preparatory school on the East Coast, had not cried when he was first born. Eric was six years younger, and the place they came from was rural enough that it wasn't because they couldn't get his mother to a doctor—it was simply what you did, mothers had their babies at home, and doctors would bring their tools and a midwife would come to help things along. He remembered the blood, the same way that Monty had remembered the blood.

It had astonished him, when Monty told that story, that they shared this bond—that they had both watched their younger siblings be born, even though men—and especially children—were not supposed to be anywhere near the birthing room. Monty remembered blood; Chuck remembered silence. "Why isn't he crying?" his mother asked frantically. "Oh God, his lips are blue."

Eric had cried after a few minutes, of course, and was a healthy kid, stronger than Chuck had been in those days. He would do well in their small Iowan town, helping to run their father's business. Was that all sons were good for? Running their fathers' business?

Was that all Mousy had been afraid of—running his father's business? Chuck couldn't claim to understand the games the wealthier boys at St. Joseph's had to play; he had to play a game of his own, to wriggle his way up the ladder—probably by kicking those a few rungs down, trying to do the same thing he was trying to do. He wasn't sure he was cut out for being a lawyer, or a doctor, or a salesman, or doing anything other than sitting in a quiet room and reading. That's where he should've stayed tonight, that quiet room.

Maybe he'd become a professor. Would his father be proud of him then? Teach at someplace like St. Joseph's, or better yet, somewhere like Princeton or Yale. He was smart enough for it, and it paid, or so he assumed. It wasn't the life his father wanted him to live, but maybe there'd come a point where he'd stop caring about that.

Maybe he wouldn't have time. Two short years till he turned eighteen—he could be drafted. All of them could. And their lives could end in a grimy trench, rain falling over their heads like God weeping, peering over the barricade to see the enemy without getting shot themselves. Would their fathers be proud of them then, in the rain, in the muck, in the dirt?

◆

He explained the situation in the morning. James was quiet, nursing his hangover, preparing for the trip home. Monty was visibly upset, saying things like "search party" and "track him down." When his agitation became physical, when he began to shake, James reached up to put a hand on his shoulder. "He's too far gone, love," he said.

He must've assumed Chuck already knew. Or he was too hungover to care. Or he was rubbing it in Chuck's face.

The headmaster questioned them extensively. What had they been doing in the forest without any adult supervision? Where had they gotten the booze? (Monty was definitely going to get in trouble for that at some point, but there were more urgent matters at hand.) Where had Andrew Carlisle gone?

"You know," Chuck said later, the three of them in the dorm room, James and Monty lying next to each other on Monty's bed, "I didn't even know his real name."

"His father will track him down before he enlists," Monty said, but he didn't sound sure of it. "He has—you know—resources."

"You mean he has money."

"Money can solve a lot of problems."

"Not all of them."

"Most."

James had been quiet ever since they'd gotten back. They were confined to their dorms for the week, outside of classes; they didn't have much to do except talk to each other, but mostly it had been Monty and Chuck talking and James just lying there, staring at the ceiling. Chuck got a sick kind of satisfaction out of that, as if something, finally, had gotten through all James's sourness and bitterness and jealousy and made him pay attention to something real. A silence stretched out so long that Chuck thought it might last forever, and then James spoke.

"You think it was my fault? For pushing him?"

"You didn't mean it," Monty said.

"Didn't I?"

"Nothing would've stopped him," Chuck said. "He had the plan in place already. Nothing would have stopped him."

James seemed to accept this as an answer, though Chuck wasn't sure it was enough to soothe a guilty soul. James turned over on the bed, burying his face in Monty's shoulder. Chuck had never noticed before how much they seemed to need each other. How they fit together, curled up like that. They must have lain together that way a million times when the dorm room was otherwise empty, waiting to spring apart at a moment's notice if Chuck or Mousy—Andrew—opened the door.

"You ever think about running away?" Chuck asked.

"Mm?" Monty had his hand tangled in James's hair; he didn't seem to be thinking about anything else.

"Running away. Being together somewhere."

They were openly acknowledging it now, apparently. If either boy was surprised that Chuck had figured it out, they didn't show it. James said nothing, just nestled his head against Monty.

"There's nowhere to run," Monty said, serious for once.

"Sure there is. Go to Iowa. Be the two old friends who run a haberdashery together. Share an apartment in the city. Bachelors do that sometimes."

"Caesar's son must be beyond reproach," James mumbled.

It seemed to Chuck that there had to be some way. That there had to be a happy ending to this story, that a year from now, they weren't all going to be in the trenches anyway, probably dead long before they turned thirty.

"Why can't any of us be happy?" he asked desperately.

Monty lifted his head, looked at him. "Because it's a rotten world," he said, "and there are more people willing to accept it for what it is than there are willing to change it."

"So change it."

"I'm outnumbered. And I'm not one of the brave ones."

"You think we'll even find out if he dies?" James asked. "Will he use his real name to enlist? He's lying about his age."

"We could write him," Monty said.

"Where would we send it?" Chuck said. "We don't know where he's going."

"So we probably won't find out when he dies."

"If he dies," Monty said.

Monty lay back again, holding James in his arms. James had closed his eyes; Monty resumed stroking his hair. The February rain tapped against the window, the sky outside gloomy and gray. Chuck got up from his desk chair, having long since given up on Homer—surely they'd give him an extension—and lifted his comforter, crawling underneath it. On a day like this, it seemed there was nothing you could do but sleep.

"Someday," Chuck said, "we're going to be the ones in charge," for the first time counting himself among the "we."

"And things will change?" James mumbled.

"And things will change."

Monty yawned. "Wake me when they do, won't you?"

Chuck understood, a little bit, what Mousy meant. How it felt not to feel alive. He hugged his comforter close to his chest and breathed in the scent of clean linen. When he dreamed, he dreamed of leathery wings and sharp, sharp teeth—being expelled from your mother's womb, screeching, and flying far, far, far away.

[POETRY]

Mosaic II

By: MuizỌpéyẹmí Àjàyí

i.
it's not so much that winter reached into my enamel
& shuddered. quarantine forming layers of husk over skin.
body mistaking silence for misanthropism.
my virtual therapist reiterates how to survive the quiet.
to perceive the globe from a glass prism.
except that the body is the crystal thickening
with distance. each wall of the mirror
cracking from our collective loss.

ii.
2 years since lagos highways were last unflocked. deserted as
anunuebe the evil tree no crow perches on.
balogun market once again smears my skin with strangers'
sweat. market women's shoe sole imprinted on my waxed loafers.
àgòyìn beans joint bubbling with steam & smoke.
i am here, happening. waiting for death to rescind the scene
where it unsheathes its scythe & munir evaporates into dawn's mist.

iii.
here, darling.
douse my wound in araldite. i promise,
the mirror gleams brightest when you leave
its scab to dry out in noonlight.

iv.
& what is it with burning that feels so similar to song?
fire. music. each torches your limb & invites you

to dance. flowing body, soluble as soda ash.
before music melts it into lime & polymer fusion. you stare
into the mirror crafted of your body &
project your silence, its iris vast & blue as the ocean
gleaming in the reflection.

v.
to be something so fragile. to know you're capable of living
is a testament you're subject to falling. how the òdèrè bird
takes to flight in spite of the huntsman's arrow.
how night sheds its skin, purple dawn
breaking to see daylight.

vi.
darling, here you are again, fracturing
my silence. it is not so much that i was unwrecked
by the storm. but i see my visage in the splintered convex
mirror. & i am not the reflection.
i am the shard of glass hanging loosely by the frame.
shrapnels. coastal shells. shattered song. impatient for sunlight.
collaging itself by the tender moonlight pouring like a creek
brimming with milk, over the glinting mosaic.

To Cut The Rot From The Fruit
McKenzie Watson-Fore

[NONFICTION]

I'm trying to develop new rhythms now that I'm back in Colorado, so I start going to the gym. Planet Fitness anchors yet another shopping plaza that I know all too well from a decade prior. My brothers and I used to buy frozen lemonade concentrate for our driveway lemonade stand from the Safeway in the center. Almost every other retail slot in the complex has cycled through tenants since I was last here. What's now a Burger King used to be a Blockbuster where I watched one of my church leaders double over with laughter when he saw *Dogma* was shelved in the comedy section. Even though I was steeped in it, I didn't know what "dogma" meant. Before the gym opened, this place was a Hobby Lobby, crafting and decorating haven for Midwest Christian mothers. Next door used to be a

Big Lots, but the light in the L burned out early, so if you drove past the plaza at night, the neon sign glowed BIGOTS.

I stand on the sidewalk in the annihilating sun and download the necessary app on my phone. The gym has its own complex ritual of admission and approval, which calls to mind the for-credit chapel services I was required to attend at my Christian college. When I duck into the atrium, my vision disappears in the sudden, enveloping darkness. I swipe my phone in front of the red-eyed QR code reader, pretending I don't feel as out of place as an octopus groping along the sand. After a moment, the dim shapes of workout machines fuzz into view.

Equipment stands in long lines, like a drone army that's all appendages, no heads. Each machine waits to be mounted. One ponytailed woman pushes the handles of an elliptical machine, which levers her feet back and forth below. A pair of buff guys spot each other on some complex torture machine in the back corner.

Gyms, I figure, are the place where people listen to podcasts, so to support this new workout habit, I've downloaded "The Rise and Fall of Mars Hill." The podcast chronicles the story of the Seattle-based megachurch, Mars Hill, helmed by sensational pastor Mark Driscoll.

When I was in high school, Driscoll was a theological darling. He was the face of the next generation of Neo-Calvinism, with its emphasis on depravity and predestination, and he became pretty famous in certain circles—namely circles of theology-hungry youth group kids like myself. Seattle was regarded as a godless wasteland, a snaggletooth protruding from the Western lip of the United States, until this young, fresh-faced pastor showed up with a passion for his city and a plan to save it by discipling men into strong fathers who led strong families.

It's difficult to overstate the cultural sway that Driscoll had. He was like a god. His aggressive ethos was a reaction against the compromises of "seeker-friendliness," a movement after 9/11 to make Christianity more palatable to the average American looking for an overarching moral framework. That framework couldn't be too demanding, harsh, or violent, or it would push those seekers away. Therefore, "seeker-friendly" churches downplayed sin, punishment, and damnation, and focused on divine love and harmony. Mark Driscoll, by contrast, disdained the seeker-friendly movement and specifically emphasized the parts of the gospel that newcomers might find repellent. He argued that seeker friendliness was cowardice, and true believers wouldn't be afraid of pushing people away. Liberal theology was watered-down. The more off-putting a belief to the uninitiated, the higher its truth value. My friends and I—teenage extremists—fell for it. We believed he was a pastor who could redeem Christianity to a skeptical and calloused generation.

Mars Hill was never my church; I've never even been to Seattle. None of the churches I've belonged to have been megachurches. None of my churches have imploded after a pastoral scandal like the one that finally ousted Mark Driscoll. But there's something about listening to this saga now, this saga of faith and personal investment followed by destruction and emotional fallout, that feels intimately connected to my own story.

I stack weights on the shoulder press and turn up the volume in my headphones. Mike Cosper, the podcast host, provides an overview of the church's gruesome end. In 2014, Driscoll resigned amidst a storm of accusations that he'd created a toxic culture. The pastor had always been an iconoclast and a firebrand, but the elder board finally decided that the characteristics that rocketed him to fame were also undermining his integrity. After a few sets of repetitions (weight training language I barely recall from required high school P.E. classes), I wipe down the machine and select a different muscle group to exercise.

Cosper mentions that many people learned about Mark Driscoll after he appeared in Donald Miller's 2003 book, *Blue Like Jazz: Nonreligious Thoughts on Christian Spirituality*. Miller referred to Driscoll as "Mark the Cussing Pastor." The reference to Donald Miller catapults me back to a different time, alongside gunmetal gray lockers in the dour, windowless hallways of my high school.

🌑

When I was in tenth grade, *Blue Like Jazz* seeped into our youth group subculture like fluoride in soil. Jonathan Presley started toting it around—and Jonathan's opinion of something set the gold standard for my evangelical friends and me. As our youth group worship band leader, Jonathan was revered for his taste in music (mostly Christian metal bands like Underoath), his fashion sense (he wore a black leather jacket to school every day), and his awareness of contemporary theologians (he kept a copy of Wayne Grudem's *Systematic Theology*—250 pages long—in the wheel-well of his Chevy GeoPrizm). If Jonathan Presley was into something, we all wanted to be into it.

In those days, my reading tastes oscillated between the Christian teen girl fiction I hoarded from the church library and French literary classics: *Les Misérables*, *The Hunchback of Notre Dame*, *The Count of Monte Cristo*. Miller's conversational prose style and first-person narration tugged me into a fully habitable world that, for the first time, resembled my own. According to Miller, Christianity—God, even—responded to the human struggle in a way that was intimate and vulnerable: "as if something was broken in the world and we were supposed to hold our palms against the wound."

We passed around dog-eared, heavily annotated copies in the darkened backstage during theater rehearsals and in the chandelier-lit foyers of suburban houses where we met for midweek youth group. Donald Miller—a pudgy white guy with a degree in sociology and a tendency to self-deprecate—became our unlikely patron saint of ordinary believers. We called him Don. We believed we could be friends. If we were to go to Portland, we could find him sitting by the front window in the coffee shops he named in his books, and we could sit down and talk to him about Jesus and beauty and longing. One of the other girls at youth group told me she would marry Donald Miller if she could.

But there was so much that we didn't know about the icons of our adolescent faith. Driscoll floated like a cloud in our ideological atmosphere, an unexamined icon for a toxic belief system I hope I would've rejected if I'd known what it entailed. I foolishly assumed the passive misogyny that saturated the environment was innocuous. Miller didn't mention it in *Blue Like Jazz*, but Driscoll led an explicitly patriarchal church. He espoused violent theology rooted in a hyper-masculine God. In a 2006 interview with *Christianity Today*, Driscoll said: "Reformed theology offers certainty, with a masculine God who names our sin, crushes Jesus on the cross for it, and sends us to hell if we fail to repent."

As far as I can remember, the leaders at my church never openly denigrated women, but we adhered, as Driscoll did, to complementarianism: the theological framework that men and women are inherently different and complementary. We never discussed the fact that "separate but equal" structures assume one group's inferiority. I didn't yet know about the progressive evangelical blogger Rachel Held Evans, who took issue with Driscoll's rampant misogyny and crude sermons, which were often littered with harsh comments and graphic sexual content.

Because conservative evangelicalism was the water in which I swam, I didn't think to question it. Critical thinking wasn't a skill we valued. Obedience was. I memorized the talking points to refute critiques of Christianity so that I never had to take the critiques seriously.

❦

I leave the gym with ten minutes left in the first episode of the podcast. One headphone is still in my ear; the other dangles on my chest. Outside, the metal of my car door handle singes my fingertips and the seatbelt sticks to my chest. The inside of the vehicle feels like a sauna but I leave the windows up and the A/C off so I can hear better.

"The Mars Hill story doesn't happen in a vacuum," host Mike Cosper says. I keep listening as I pull my car onto the two-lane highway and head west toward the mountains. He begins to list other pastors who lost their pulpits as a result of moral scandal. Bill Hybels resigned from megachurch Willow Creek after allegations of sexual assault. Perry Noble was removed from megachurch NewSpring Church for alcoholism and family neglect. Tullian Tchividijian left multiple churches after multiple inappropriate sexual relationships with congregants. Ted Haggard, former president of the National Association of Evangelicals, was fired from multiple churches after incidents of drug use and inappropriate sexual relationships with young men. Carl Lentz, fired from megachurch Hillsong NYC for poor leadership and infidelity; James MacDonald, fired from megachurch Harvest Bible Church for abuses of power; and finally, Ravi Zacharias, called "the greatest Christian apologist of this century" by former Vice President Mike Pence, who headlined a weeklong chapel intensive at my college and was later exposed for sexually assaulting numerous women and instructing them to stay silent, lest they jeopardize the faith of millions. Sweat condenses in my armpits and edges the seams of my tank top. My whole body feels slick and salinated. "These are celebrity names, but this is far from just a celebrity problem," the host continues. "It seems like it's an epidemic."

A liquid bead drips from my chin onto my shirt, leaving a small wet spot. It's not sweat. I'm crying. Without me even noticing, my eyes filled up, and now tears are running down my face unimpeded, like spring snowmelt down the side of a mountain. I can't stop the tears. Alone in my car, I don't want to. My fingers tighten around the steering wheel. The skin pulls taut over my knuckles and tears drop onto my thighs where my gym shorts are riding up and a cache of sadness rips open inside of me. My eyes are sweating grief.

So many pastors. So much damage. So much grief.

Ed Stetzer, an executive at *Christianity Today*, adds his baritone to the podcast.

"There's a body count," he says, "of young pastors whose ability rose them to prominence before their character was ready for it." Without moving my eyes from the road, I thumb the pause button on my phone and fixate on the painted white lines while Stetzer's words reverberate in my ear. *A body count.* Of the pastors. Those poor young pastors, Stetzer seems to say. The well inside me seems to double, as if a false bottom caved in, and the tears come so thick and fast I can barely see the road. If these pastors were the men who were supposed to lead us, what do people think is happening to those of us who tried to follow them?

I am not crying for the pastors who have fallen but for the empty space in my chest I fear will never be filled again. Christianity was meant to fill "a God-shaped hole" inside of me, and I still have the hole, this basketball-sized cavity behind my ribs, but evangelicalism no longer fills it. It's a breach in my self-coherence, and the void threatens to engulf me.

．

When I was a child, I saw faith through the lens of all-encompassing truth. Everything I did and thought and felt corresponded to it. My weekly schedule was built around church on Sunday and midweek youth group. I studied the Bible, dressed modestly, and evaluated culture with my Christian values. Church gave me a level of security, stability, and clarity few kids get to know. Evangelicalism was my whole world, and I had no reason to question it.

I knew what was Right and Wrong, back then. I knew what I was supposed to do with my life and I felt assured that what I was doing was Good. Even if I wasn't praised for it on Earth or I sometimes felt like an outsider, I knew I would be rewarded when I got to heaven. Jesus would greet me with fond recognition and deliver the affirmation every believer hopes to hear: "Well done, good and faithful servant."

But since then, I've stacked other lenses on top of that first one, adding layers of color, distorting the base image. I went away to Christian college, where everyone showed up with slightly different versions of Christianity, and everyone thought theirs was the most right. My New Testament Survey professor lectured on early church disagreements between the Apostles Peter and Paul, Redaction Criticism—how to make sense of the "contradictions" between the synoptic gospels (Matthew, Mark, and Luke), and his theory that the resurrected Lazarus authored the fourth gospel (the one otherwise known as "John"). I became close friends with a girl who believed that true believers should be able to speak in tongues, and though I prayed and prayed for that "baptism of the Spirit," I never received it. When I came back home for Christmas Break, I filled the insert of my church program with notes, but they were mostly scribbled wonderings if I fit there anymore.

One day in Houston a few years ago, I bussed past South Main Baptist Church, and their black and white welcome sign took my breath away. I'd passed it a hundred other times, but that day, their tripartite mission statement—"Worship God, Discover God's Word, and Share with Others"—transported me back to a time when faith was simple. For a brief moment, those words conjured in me the unquestioning clarity of growing up evangelical. My body recognized the call. *That's what I'm supposed to do.* Muscle memory would've walked me right into the church if I hadn't been on the bus. At Calvary—the church where I grew up—our mission was "to build Christ-centered communities of people fully devoted to loving God and loving others." I hear those words and they still click with something inside me, like a bolt falling into place, like a puzzle piece that finds its exact fit. Of course those words still resonate: I was raised to mold my personhood around that call.

I still attended Calvary intermittently when I visited from Houston. Every week, my parents sit where they've always sat: on the right side of the sanctuary, about halfway towards the front. Ellen Lundy, our old next door neighbor, usually shares their pew.

These different experiences and contexts and interpretations make me feel like I'm looking at something underwater: a little warped, a few degrees off. Some days, I wish I could go back to the simplistic security of my childhood perspective, but it's inaccessible to me now. I know I can never go back to that place of unquestioning belief. I can no longer approach faith unguarded by my shields of intellectualism, skepticism, cynicism.

I know my exile is self-imposed. No one threw me out. No ultimatums were extended, no nasty confrontations or ugly words exchanged. Now that I've moved back to Boulder, I could commute to Calvary in half the time; I could attend Sunday service this week and no one would blink an eye.

Instead of returning to Calvary, I return to the gym, where the podcast fuels my workouts with fury. I shoulder-press stacks of weights and exhale rage. I do lat-pull-downs and bicep curls and hand weights, all while listening to podcast host Mike Cosper analyze Mars Hill's church branding, use of war metaphor, and pastoral power struggles. I shoulder press to information about religious subjugation of women and spiritual abuse. My thighs bulge and push pounds of resistance to the end of the leg press machine and back, to the end and back, to the end and back.

Evangelicalism erupts year after year with scandal as another prominent preacher falls. These pastors, "men of God," crumple in their roles and hurl collateral damage in every direction like a whirling dervish of pain, and still women are considered unfit to preach? Men dominate the system that taught me to override my own instincts and defer my authority. My muscles quiver with exertion. I am furious with Mike Cosper for his ability to tell this story in a measured tone of voice. I am furious with Mark Driscoll and furious with every church elder who enabled him. I am furious with this system that refuses to learn from its serial failures, this system for which it seems the victim count will never be high enough to compel change, furious with myself for thinking the goodness outweighed the cost.

On each drive home, sweat percolates inside my sports bra and drips down my temples and the anger unclenches and softens into a bottomless grief in my belly. I drive home and cry—because I want it all to be true. Not the scandal, not the abuses of power or the diminishment of women. I want evangelicalism to be true, in all its deferred glory, so I could just go on believing what I was raised to believe. I want to be able to return: to be welcomed back into the place I knew as home, and to feel any dissonance dissolve like powder in water. I want to feel as uncomplicated in calling church home as I did when I was young. I want to feel the absolute clarity and purpose that I used to feel when standing in the sanctuary for worship. I want to feel nothing but fondness toward the belief system with which I grew up.

This nostalgia-grief makes me want to reach back to a previous version of myself who doesn't exist anymore.

Everything would be so much easier if evangelicalism was not as flawed as the men who failed. I want the comfort of believing that we can cut out the rot and go on eating the fruit.

But now I feel so lost and I feel so angry and these feelings seem endless.

The dissonance persists. I can't turn it all back. I can't wish it all away. Not without turning myself inside out, erasing my inner knowing once again.

❧

On my drive home from the gym, acres of farmland spill away from the road. Rows of leafy cottonwood trees mark drainage ditches that crisscross pale green pastures. The men on the podcast continue to ponder this rash of pastoral failure and their male voices fall away from me as I wonder: what if the problem isn't restricted to bad actors? What if the system produces so many bad actors because it breeds and rewards bad behavior—unchecked power, arrogance, and domination, a narrative of redemptive violence, unlimited forgiveness for past wrongs? Which is really to ask—are the abuses a fluke, or are they a feature? Can the goodness that I experienced be separated from religious harm?

I don't want to have to reckon with my own beliefs—to probe through them like documents in an archive, retraining myself to recognize how the theology I accepted fed and fueled abuse. How have my beliefs, too, contributed to this epidemic? Where have I been complicit?

My Honda zips along the country road, past the occasional duck pond and stone-flanked entrances to semi-rural subdivisions. Someone plotted this land on a map. They coded which sections would be agricultural and residential, which portions of earth would be dedicated to each purpose. But what if the residential tract was somehow compromised: undermined by a hidden floodplain, an unknown sinkhole?

I wish I could take the material of my faith and spread it out before me, and there was some tool I could use to carve it up, marking which parts are good and which are bad: which to embrace and which to jettison. To separate the wheat from the chaff. This is what my faith taught me to do: to look at the world and splice away sacred from secular, to fraternize exclusively with Christian kids and to "minister to" the nonbelievers, to elevate the virtuous and avoid even the appearance of evil. The Apostle Paul exhorted believers to think on that which is good, true, and righteous, but to do so requires a hermeneutic to distinguish between the good and bad.

What if our method for determining good and bad was also flawed? What if you teach someone to lift weights but you teach them wrong, and with each repetition, they're hurting themselves?

The evangelical church in America is a massive system of power and hierarchy, influence and indoctrination. Those who ushered me into it did so because they believed it would benefit me as it had them. My mentors, my youth leaders, even my parents—I know to the core of my being that they meant no harm. But that doesn't erase the damage. The presence of good intentions doesn't eradicate the reality of harm.

This is the hard part. This is the news I wish I didn't have to break, the news that is breaking me.

Evangelicalism preaches that all can be redeemed. But growing up evangelical was an experience less redemptive than ruinous. I don't want to admit this. For weeks of gym workouts, the podcast trickles through my ears and I shove the weight away and when I am depleted and exhausted from the effort, I cry in the solace of my sauna-like SUV on the way home. The two halves of my ribcage try to peel away from each other, threatening to rip me in half if it means I can maintain the facade of health, if I can pretend that the church didn't wound me more than it healed. I want to punch through a window, to shatter something other than my own fragile narrative that it wasn't so bad. Nothing that a good attitude and a focus on the positives can't fix—or at least, nothing I can't overlook for the sake of maintaining the faith's reputation.

I wish evangelicalism was as good as we believed it to be. The leadership of Mars Hill allowed Driscoll to stay in power for so long, despite concerns, because they believed the net gains outweighed the costs. But how much damage can be overlooked? Our leaders urged us—the followers, the youths, the women—to ignore the harm in favor of greater outcomes. They assured us it would all balance out, and we believed them. But even now, the podcast focuses on the sensational pastor, and not the congregation he destroyed.

My car pulls into the cul-de-sac in front of my little yellow house. My shoulders are shaking. Flecks of sweat land like spittle on the pigmented leather of the seat. I tug my headphone out of my ear, get out of my car, and smear the backs of my thumbs across my cheekbones to wipe away the traces of tears.

[POETRY]

Yellow Prayers in the Fall Wind

By: Eli Coyle

If you walk long enough, you'll arrive
at that old oak by the umber barn

the one with the Spanish moss
overgrown and bearded
just beyond the mule deer's reach.

If you walk far enough, in time—
you'll arrive at that ancestral house,

the one with the rusted tin roof
panels on the 40-acre lot

        (home to five generations)

where my mother dreamed
of leaving that small town

out beyond the old Argonaut mine
on the slanted hills of blue oak.

There are days I think she still lives there—
in the waning growing gradually quiet

out beyond the walnut trees
walking the ochre roads into the pasture

that a part of her is at peace

with that transparent shimmer
we sometimes call God

shaking loose
the yellow prayers

of maple leaves
in the fall wind

sometimes answered
in ordinary ways.

[CONTRIBUTORS]

FICTION

Page 8
Ashley Bao is a Chinese-Canadian-American writer currently attending Amherst College. Her poetry and short fiction have appeared in *Reckoning*, *Strange Horizons*, *Cast of Wonders*, and elsewhere. She may sometimes be found looking at cute cats on X @ashleybaozi

Page 26
Serena Paver (she/they) is a queer dance/movement psychotherapist, writer, and embodied creator. Born and raised in Cape Town, South Africa, and based in London, Serena's work centers on the body, mental health, (mis)communication, and human connection, and has been published in *Transnationalism*, *The Foreigner Press*, and *Roey Writes On*.

Page 40
M.K. Opar is a non-denominational church employee by day and a writer by night. She lives with her family in North Metro Atlanta and recently graduated from Kennesaw State University with a bachelor's in psychology and a minor in religious studies. "Miss Helmet-Head" is her first literary publication.

Page 58
Kelsey Myers holds an MFA in creative nonfiction from Columbia University. Her work has appeared in *The Write Launch*. She and her wife reside in the Rust Belt of Ohio.

NONFICTION

Page 52
Belinda J. Kein is an expat New Yorker who resides in San Diego, CA. A poet early on, she now brings her lyricism and love of the succinct to short fiction, creative nonfiction, and hybrid prose. Her work has appeared in *The Fourth River*, *The Razor*, *2022 Dime Stories Anthology*, *Mom Egg Review*, *The New York Times* and *The Spirit of Pregnancy*. Additionally, her work is scheduled to appear in *Hippocampus Magazine*, *Vestal Review* and the *Stanchion Away From Home Anthology*. She holds an MA in English from San Diego State University and an MFA in fiction from Queens University of Charlotte. She is currently working on a flash collection.

Page 80
McKenzie Watson-Fore is a writer, artist, and critic based in her hometown of Boulder, Colorado. She holds an MFA in writing from Pacific University and is working on a collection of essays about white American evangelicalism and the female experience. Her work has been published or is forthcoming in *Write or Die Magazine*, *Psaltery & Lyre*, *CALYX*, and elsewhere. She can be found at MWatsonFore.com or drinking tea on her back porch.

POETRY

Page 6
Alyssa Stadtlander is a writer and actress based in Boise, Idaho. Her work is published in *Ekstasis*, *Mudfish Magazine*, *Fathom*, and others, along with several anthologies, including *An Homage to Soren Kierkegaard: A Poetry Anthology*, edited by Dana Gioia and Mary Grace Mangano. She is the recipient of the 16th Annual Mudfish Magazine Poetry Prize, judged by Marie Howe. For more, visit her website at www.alyssastadtlander.com

Page 25
Nathanael O'Reilly is the author of twelve poetry collections, including *Dublin Wandering*, *Landmarks*, *Selected Poems of Ned Kelly*, *Boulevard*, *(Un)belonging* and *Preparations for Departure*. His poetry appears in journals & anthologies published in fifteen countries. He is the poetry editor for *Antipodes: A Global Journal of Australian/New Zealand Literature*.

Page 56
Rebecca Pyle is an American writer who has been living in France over the past year. Her poetry is published in *Chattahoochee Review*, *Penn Review*, and *Anacapa Review*; fiction by her appears in *The Los Angeles Review* and *Pangyrus Literary*. Once upon a time she was a runner-up in the United Kingdom's National Poetry Competition and the winner of the Carruth poetry prize. Artwork by her also appears in many art/lit journals, including *The Rathalla Review*, *Blood Orange Review*, and *New England Review*. See rebeccapyleartist.com

Page 78
Muiz Ọpẹ́yẹmí Àjàyí (Frontier XVIII) is an editor at *The Nigeria Review*, poetry reader for *Adroit Journal*, and a 2023 Poetry Translation Centre UNDERTOW cohort. Winner of the Lagos-London Poetry Competition 2022, University of Ibadan Law LDS Poetry Prize 2022, shortlisted/longlisted for Ake Poetry Prize, Briefly Write Poetry Prize, Kreative Diadem Poetry Prize, a Best of The Net nominee, he features in *Frontier Poetry*, *Chestnut Review*, *20.35 Africa: An Anthology of Contemporary Poetry*, *Tab Journal*, *Olongo Africa*, *Lolwe*, *SAND Journal*, *Poetry Wales*, *Aké Review*, *Yabaleft Review*, *Poetry Column-NND*, and elsewhere.

Page 92
Eli Coyle holds a MA in English from California State University, Chico and an MFA in creative writing from the University of Nevada, Reno. His poetry and prose have recently been published or are forthcoming in: *Harpur Palate*, *New York Quarterly*, *The Normal School*, *Poet Lore*, *Sierra Nevada Review*, and *The South Carolina Review* among others. He currently teaches in the English Department at the University of Nevada, Reno.